Reaching Out, Royce Sought Julia's Face.

She trembled, but didn't turn away.

Clichéd phrases—*velvet-soft, satin-smooth*—sleeted through Royce's brain. None of them adequately described the exquisite texture of Julia Kendrick's skin.

Emboldened, he lifted his left hand and cupped the right side of her face. Again, he felt her tremble. Again, she didn't turn away.

Yes, he thought. At long last, he could *see* her, if only in his mind's eye. The curve of her forehead, the arch of her brows, the length and thickness of her lashes...

And her mouth!

"Please..." he suddenly heard her whisper. Her warm breath misted on his knuckles. "Oh, please..." A moment later, he felt her fingers curl up and over his wrists.

And then he did something he'd wanted to do from the first time he heard her voice. He kissed her....

Dear Reader,

I know this is a hectic time of year. From the moment you cut into that Thanksgiving turkey, to the second midnight chimes on December 31, life is one nonstop *RUSH*. But don't forget to take some private time…and relax with Silhouette Desire!

We begin with *An Obsolete Man*, a marvelous *Man of the Month* from the ever-entertaining Lass Small. Next we have *The Headstrong Bride*, the latest installment in Joan Johnston's CHILDREN OF HAWK'S WAY series.

And there's *Hometown Wedding*, the first book in a fun-filled new series, JUST MARRIED, by Pamela Macaluso, a talented new-to-Desire writer. And speaking of new authors, don't miss Metsy Hingle's debut title, *Seduced*.

This month is completed with *Dark Intentions*, a sensuous, heartwarming love story by Carole Buck, and *Murdock's Family*, a powerfully dramatic offering by Paula Detmer Riggs.

Happy holidays—don't worry, you'll survive them!

Lucia Macro
Senior Editor

Please address questions and book requests to:
Silhouette Reader Service
U.S.: 3010 Walden Ave., P.O. Box 1325, Buffalo, NY 14269
Canadian: P.O. Box 609, Fort Erie, Ont. L2A 5X3

CAROLE BUCK
DARK INTENTIONS

SILHOUETTE *Desire*®
Published by Silhouette Books
America's Publisher of Contemporary Romance

SILHOUETTE BOOKS

ISBN 0-373-05899-3

DARK INTENTIONS

Copyright © 1994 by Carol Buckland

Printed in U.S.A.

CAROLE BUCK

is a television news writer and movie reviewer who lives in Atlanta. She is single, and her hobbies include cake decorating, ballet and traveling. She collects frogs but does not kiss them. Carole says she's in love with life; she hopes the books she writes reflect this.

Prologue

Royce Archer Williams confronted the possibility of death the way he was accustomed to dealing with life.

Head-on. By himself. In a hurry.

He recognized that what was about to happen was his fault. He'd been driving too fast. He always drove too fast when he was alone. And "alone" was how he preferred to be.

Royce was aware that those who knew him maintained he did a great many things too quickly. Too carelessly. He was essentially indifferent to these characterizations of his behavior.

His existence wasn't predicated on a need to win other people's approval or affection. With a few notable exceptions, he didn't give a damn what other people said or did or felt. Nor did he expect other people to give a damn what *he* said or did or felt. Unless he paid them to do so, of course. In that case, he demanded full value for his money.

Royce pumped his brakes carefully, trying to steer out of the skid. For one heart-stopping instant the wheels seemed to catch and hold on to the slippery surface of the highway. But it was only for an instant.

It was a pity about the car, he thought suddenly. It was a beautiful vehicle. A genuine work of art. That was one of the reasons he'd willingly spent a fortune to possess it. The other was that it was flashy and foreign, two qualities his late, unlamented father had always despised.

His father. Lord! He wouldn't put it past the old bastard to be glaring up from hell at this very moment and—

Royce Williams's fine, flashy, foreign car smashed into the embankment that ran along the right side of the road. In the first excruciating split second of impact, a decade-old image exploded in his brain.

Eyes.

Exquisite, aquamarine eyes.

Eyes that pleaded with him from a bleeding, brutalized face. Eyes that probed to the depths of his sorely battered soul and, astoundingly, did not seem to find him wanting as a human being.

"Don't," the child-woman to whom those unique, blue-green eyes belonged had begged him on a frigid winter evening some ten years ago. "Please. D-don't . . . g-go."

He'd promised her he wouldn't. But in the end, he had. He'd left without a word and he'd never looked back.

Until now, when it was too late.

God.

Too late for him to—

Oh . . . God.

Royce Archer Williams's world went black.

Julia Kendricks blinked against the dazzling light of the noonday sun.

Not like this, she protested silently. Her throat ached. Her eyes stung with unshed tears. Dear Lord, I never wanted it to be like this!

Julia blinked a second time, then turned her attention back to the newspaper she was holding. Swallowing hard, she stared at the front-page photograph of a face she knew at least as well as her own. After a few moments she began rereading the double-columned story that accompanied it.

The article was datelined Boston, October 27.

Royce A. Williams, 36, owner and CEO of the Boston-based investment firm Williams Venture, Inc., was injured last night in an automobile accident.

Julia drew a shaky breath. Her gaze skipped down the page. A few phrases leapt out with crystalline clarity.

...head injuries...loss of vision, according to Dr. Dennis Mitchell, Williams's personal physician.

Julia clutched the paper against her and closed her eyes. The past rushed in to claim her.

She remembered the cold. And the shame.

She remembered the fear. And the pain.

"It's all right," a man she'd never met, whose name she hadn't learned until after he'd gone away, had told her. Then he'd taken one of her hands in his, gently enveloping her filthy, broken-nailed fingers with his strong, clean ones.

His touch had warmed her to the very center of her soul. For a tiny moment in time she'd forgotten the cold, the shame, the fear and the pain, and she'd glimpsed a future that seemed worth living.

"You're safe now," he'd gone on to say. "Help is on the way."

Julia opened her eyes. She could feel herself trembling.

Ten years, she thought. For more than ten years she'd waited....

She'd never wanted it to be like this. Not like *this!*

Julia Kendricks looked down at the newspaper photograph of Royce Archer Williams once again. "It's all right," she whispered, touching the grainy black-and-white image with the tip of one finger. "Help is on the way."

Suddenly the sunshine seemed even brighter than before.

One

Where Royce Williams had once known light, there was now only darkness.

Hidden in the heart of this darkness was a woman named Julia Kendricks. She was a twenty-six-year-old teacher of the blind. She'd been recommended by his doctor and friend, Dennis Mitchell.

Dennis had been uncharacteristically insistent that he hire Julia Kendricks, Royce recalled. "Let her help you," his friend had urged.

Royce grimaced inwardly.

Help.

God, how he loathed that particular four-letter word and all the weaknesses it implied.

His blindness was temporary, dammit! Yes, he'd awoken to a blacked-out world on the morning of October 27th, and no, there hadn't been any discernible improvement in his condition during the five weeks since then. But neither had anyone been able to discover a single physiological reason why his sight shouldn't return.

He was going to make a full recovery. That's all there was to it. And once he recovered, he would have no need for *anybody's* help... least of all, this Julia Kendricks's.

He was prepared to give her a chance, but he knew she wouldn't last any longer than the other alleged "helpers" he'd had foisted on him. He was willing to bet Dennis's protégée would be gone from his Commonwealth Avenue town house within days and totally forgotten shortly after that.

Royce rubbed his chin, considering. Well... maybe not *totally* forgotten, he conceded. No matter that the woman now sitting across from him had intruded on his sightless existence barely forty minutes ago. Something about her had gotten to him at a very elemental level within the first few moments of their meeting.

Royce shifted uncomfortably in his chair. He'd elected to hold this interview in his study. Of all the rooms in his town house, this was the one where he retained the greatest sense of control. Although he'd been out of the hospital for nearly three weeks, the rest of his home still seemed alien to him. As for what the world *outside* his home seemed—

Lord. He didn't even want to think about that!

In his study, Royce knew precisely where everything was. Loss of vision or no, it was his turf. He could summon up a mental image of the antique walnut desk he was sitting behind and locate any of the items arranged on top of it without hesitation. Or he could step out from behind the desk, take eight strides directly forward and reach confidently for the polished knob of the door, which opened into the front entrance hall.

There was no stumbling as long as he remained in his study. No stumbling. No bumbling. And no need to go groping in the damned dark.

Royce shifted again. "Do you have any questions about the job, Miss Kendricks?"

"I don't think so, Mr. Williams," she replied. "You've made things very clear."

Royce let a few moments tick by, keeping his eyes fixed on the spot where he knew Julia was sitting. She disturbed him, this unseen woman with the mellow, musical voice. She disturbed him a great deal.

"Do you honestly believe you can teach me to accept being blind?" he abruptly demanded.

"No." The answer was quick and unequivocal.

"No?"

"Acceptance is a lesson you have to learn on your own, Mr. Williams." Julia's voice was serene. But beneath the serenity Royce could hear strength. It was as obvious as steel wiring beneath a web of silk. "Assuming you decide to learn it at all."

Royce gripped the arms of his chair, struggling with a sudden surge of anger. Was this woman *judging* him?

"What if I don't decide to learn, Miss Kendricks?" he challenged.

"I . . ." For the first time since the start of the interview, there was a hint of hesitation. "I can't answer that."

Royce leaned forward, sensing weakness and automatically seeking to take advantage of it. "Just what *can* you do?"

Another hint of hesitation. Then, astonishingly, "I can teach you how to avoid tripping over furniture and walking into walls."

It took Royce a second or two to accept that Julia had actually said what he thought she'd said. Once he did, he came within a hairbreadth of losing his temper. The words "get out" trembled on the tip of his tongue.

He never uttered the command. An odd jolt of emotion—could it be admiration for her nerve?—caused him to swallow it whole.

Royce Williams would be the first to admit that he'd never been easy to deal with. He would also admit that his wealth and position generally tended to insulate him against complaints about his temperament and manners. Yet in the wake of his accident, he'd gradually become aware that a lot of people were allowing him to behave in ways he knew damn well they never would have tolerated if he'd still been able to see.

They meant well, these people. Royce didn't doubt for an instant that they were sincere in their solicitous assurances and sympathetic offers of aid. But because of these well-meaning individuals, he'd endured more than a month of receiving the same pernicious message over and over.

The gist of this message: that he was diminished by his disability and had to be coddled accordingly.

Julia's response to his deliberately offensive inquiry communicated something very different. In one short sentence she'd made it plain that if he was going to toss down verbal gauntlets around her, he'd better be ready to have them flung back in his face. Others might excuse rudeness, or worse, because of his blindness. Julia apparently didn't intend to.

Royce got to his feet. Sounds from the other side of the desk told him that she was standing, too.

"Mr. Williams—" she began. There was a tremor in her voice Royce hadn't heard before. He discovered he didn't like the sound of it one bit.

"Emerson will show you upstairs," he interrupted. "We can start the furniture avoidance lessons as soon as you're settled."

Julia slowly surveyed the high-ceilinged, ivory-and-roses bedroom suite that had been designated as hers. Everything in the place—from the needlepointed rugs to the elegantly proportioned antique furniture—spoke of exquisite taste and the wherewithal to indulge it. Yet instead of being intimidating, the overall effect was wonderfully soothing.

"Soothing" was definitely something she needed, Julia acknowledged. The interview she'd just gone through had been much more stressful than she'd anticipated.

She'd realized the situation was going to be difficult, of course, Dr. Mitchell had been extremely frank about that. But nothing he'd said—and none of the scenarios she'd envisioned—had prepared her for the sledgehammer impact of finally meeting the man who'd literally rescued her out of a gutter.

She'd been trembling when she'd been shown into Royce Williams's study a little less than an hour ago. The awful ambivalence she'd experienced when she'd learned about his accident had been roiling within her.

Her first glimpse of Royce had compounded her emotional tumult. Although she'd collected several dozen pictures of him over the years, some irrational corner of her mind had expected his appearance to conform with an image that was more than a decade old.

The scattered strands of silver at his temples had surprised her. So, too, the fine web of wrinkles radiating from the corners of his deep-set, thickly lashed eyes and the grooves bracketing his wide, flexible mouth.

More shocking than the inevitable indications of aging had been the anger she'd seen. Royce Williams had looked like a man being eaten alive by rage.

Her impulse—visceral, almost irresistible—had been to embrace him the way she would a child. She'd wanted to reach out and offer him the same unconditional comfort he'd once offered her.

Fortunately something inside her had managed to quell this impulse. And for this, Julia was profoundly grateful. Instinct told her that no matter how badly Royce Archer Williams was handling the loss of his sight, his response to anything remotely resembling pity would likely be much worse.

In a flash, she'd settled on a strategy. Her manner toward him would be professional and impersonal. She would be pleasant. But if he pushed her, she would push back.

She'd managed to sustain this ploy until the very end of the interview. Royce's reaction to her comment about the tripping over furniture and walking into walls had broken her nerve. The expression she'd seen in his dark, sightless eyes had shaken her. She'd been afraid. But her fear had been more for him than for herself.

Then something had changed. She'd sensed it even as she'd begun to apologize. One second Royce had plainly been on the verge of throwing her out. The next he'd been telling her that Emerson would escort her—

"Miss Kendricks?"

Julia started. She took a moment to compose herself, then turned to face the man who'd just addressed her. He was the same man who'd ushered her into Royce's study. Emerson's age was difficult to determine. He could have been anywhere from his late forties to his early sixties. Although his cropped iron gray hair and craggy face argued for the latter, the quiet vigor of his movements suggested a man whose prime was more than a memory.

"Yes?" she responded.

"Is there a problem with the room?"

"A prob— Oh." Julia shook her head as she realized how her long silence had been misinterpreted. "Oh, no. Not at all. It's lovely."

Emerson regarded her without speaking for what seemed like an exceedingly long time. "This was Mrs. Williams's favorite room," he finally observed. He had a very slight Irish accent. It lent a lilting edge of poetry to his words.

Julia's gaze drifted toward the room's queen-size bed. It was draped with a luxurious-looking coverlet made of ivory linen and cutwork lace.

"Mrs. Williams?" she echoed.

"Royce's mother."

Julia experienced a curious frisson of relief. She hadn't really thought the Mrs. Williams in question was Royce's wife. Still, the newspaper stories she'd read over the years had made it clear that her former benefactor was not a self-denying monk when it came to women. So it was always possible that—

"You might have noticed her photograph," Emerson commented. "Downstairs. In the study."

Julia glanced at the older man. He was still examining her with intense and very open interest. She sustained his scrutiny for a few moments, then broke eye contact. Nibbling on her lower lip, she cast her mind back.

She hadn't really paid very much attention to Royce's study. She'd been far too concerned with him. The main thing she'd noticed about the room was how organized it seemed to be. The professional in her had approved of this. Orderliness was one of the cornerstones of providing a blind person with a sense of security. For instance, the items on the top of the desk Royce had been sitting behind had obviously been arranged—

"The picture in the silver frame," she recalled abruptly, summoning up the image of a pale, heart-shaped face surrounded by dark, wavy hair.

"Exactly."

Julia frowned, trying to focus on the photograph she'd conjured up in her mind's eye. After a few seconds she looked at Emerson once again.

"She was beautiful," she said. What she did not add was that the woman in the picture had appeared sad, too.

An odd expression moved across the older man's face like a cloud scudding in front of the moon. "Yes," he agreed quietly. "Mrs. Williams was very beautiful."

"You knew her well?" It wasn't exactly a question.

"I came to work here several years after she married Mr. Williams." It wasn't exactly an answer.

There was a pause. Eventually, Emerson did a bit of discreet throat-clearing and inquired, "Will you be needing any help in getting yourself settled, Miss Kendricks?"

Julia controlled an urge to continue probing about Royce's mother. "No, thanks," she responded. "I'll be fine."

"All right." The older man turned to go.

"Uh, Mr. Emerson?"

He pivoted to face her. "Just Emerson."

"I beg your pardon?"

"Just Emerson. Talley O'Hara Emerson. No 'Mister.'"

"Oh." Julia toyed briefly with the notion of asking him to call her by her first name, then abandoned it. She had the feeling Emerson would be less than receptive to such a request. "I see."

"I'm sure you do."

Julia took a moment to collect her thoughts. There was an issue she needed to discuss with the man standing before her. The question was, how best to broach it.

"I gather you live here," she eventually said.

Emerson nodded. "I have the top floor. There's a housekeeper. Mrs. Wolfe. She lives out. Comes in Monday through Friday after breakfast. She's got a girl to clean three times a week."

"Oh." Julia plucked a piece of lint off the front of the loose-fitting cardigan she had on, still searching for the most effective tack to take. "Uh, Mr. Williams has had other instructors, hasn't he? Since his accident, I mean. People to help him deal with the loss of his sight?"

"A few." Emerson shrugged, his mouth twisting. "None of them lasted very long."

The observation stung. Julia cocked her chin. "Yes, well, none of them was me."

Something sparked in the depths of Emerson's pale blue eyes. "I wasn't thinking they were."

Uncertain what to make of his tone, Julia decided to be direct. "Look, Emerson," she began. "I don't know what kind of arrangements you had with the other instructors, but this job is very important to me, and I'm hoping you'll be willing to help. Now, I'm not exactly sure what your responsibilities are—"

"I do whatever's necessary, Miss Kendricks," came the quiet, uncompromising reply. "And any help you might be needing from me is yours."

"So, Emerson," Royce said a few minutes later. He drummed his fingers against the top of his desk. "What do you think?"

"Of Miss Kendricks?"

"Yes."

"Intriguing."

There was a silence. During the course of it, Royce fought and lost a battle against the need to voice the question that seemed to underscore the galling nature of his current condition.

"What does she look like?" he finally asked.

"Mmm…" Emerson paused as though contemplating the matter very carefully. "She's about five foot seven. Slim but curvy where it counts. Long hair. Pale. Like strained honey."

"Blond?" Royce was surprised. Something about h... "teacher's" husky-sweet voice had made him think... might be a brunette.

"Natural, too, if I know anything. Her eyes are unusual. Midway between blue and green. Sea-colored, almost."

"In other words, she's attractive," Royce concluded brusquely, deciding to abandon the subject. Julia Kendricks's appearance, attractive or otherwise, had no more significance for him than the supposedly sublime sounds of a symphony did for a deaf man.

Of course, it *might* have some significance for Dennis Mitchell, he thought suddenly. In fact, Julia's appearance might very well be the reason why his good friend had seemed so all-fired interested—

"Definitely attractive," Emerson concurred. "But trying not to be."

"Trying not to be?" Royce echoed, startled. "What does that mean?"

There was another pause, punctuated by an odd sigh. "To tell the truth, I'm not certain I know. Maybe she's one of those women who doesn't care about clothes and cosmetics. But if I had to bet, I'd say she's downplaying—not indifferent."

"She wears perfume," Royce observed. A pang of emotion he couldn't put a name to lanced through him. He'd caught Julia's scent when they'd shaken hands at the start of their interview. Fresh and clean, like a dew-drenched spring morning, it had had little in common with the expensively alluring fragrances favored by most of the women of his acquaintance. Yet it had stirred him in ways he couldn't begin to articulate.

"Does she, now?" Emerson sounded surprised. "That, I didn't notice."

Royce leaned back in his chair and gave a brief, bitter laugh. "Maybe if I'd been able to see her, I wouldn't have, either."

Two

Royce took a step forward. He swung the cane he was holding in his right hand in a low, flat arc in front of him.

He never should have asked, he berated himself. He never—ever—should have asked what Julia Kendricks looked like.

How many times during the past two and a half weeks had he tried to conjure up an image of her? he wondered. How many times had he blended Emerson's description with his own observations about the tantalizing timbre of her voice, about the scent of her skin, about the soft feel of her—

Stop it!

Royce took a second step. Then a third. And a fourth.

He didn't want—didn't need!—to become any more involved with Julia Kendricks than he already was, he emphasized to himself. The less he knew about her, the better.

It wasn't as though he couldn't have found out all about her if he'd chosen to. As the owner and CEO of a very successful investment firm, he had the resources to discover her secrets very easily. He simply didn't choose to exercise them.

Still . . .

All right. Royce had to admit to a certain curiosity about Julia's tenacity. His assumption that she would quit within a few days of her arrival had proven faulty. The truth was, Dennis Mitchell's protégée seemed to be becoming more entrenched in his town house with each passing hour.

Heaven knew, he'd provided her with plenty of cause to storm out his front door and never return. But for reasons he couldn't fathom, she'd opted to stay put and take everything he decided to dish out.

This wasn't to suggest that Julia had lain down and played doormat for him. Quite the contrary.

Just what can *you do?* he'd demanded during their initial interview.

I can teach you how to avoid tripping over furniture and walking into walls, she'd replied.

In many ways, this brief exchange had established the basic pattern of their relationship. He'd lost track of the number of times since then that he'd goaded and Julia had responded by—

Royce collided with something. Hard. Off balance, he dropped the aluminum cane he was supposed to be learning to regard as an integral part of his life. He heard it clatter against the floor as he reached out, grabbing hold of the object he'd run into. It took him a few seconds to identify what he was clutching.

"What the hell is a dining room chair doing in the middle of this hallway?" he demanded, transforming his embarrassment into anger.

"Letting you know you're not concentrating on today's mobility exercise," came the quiet reply from a few feet behind him.

A moment later Royce heard Julia move. At least, he thought he did. Although she'd worn high-heeled shoes during their first meeting—he'd heard them click against the study's hardwood floor when she'd walked in—she'd switched to some kind of soft-soled flats once she'd started working. The change of footwear made it almost impossible for him to keep track of her when she wasn't speaking.

Perhaps this was her intention. Then again, perhaps the flats were part of the playing-down effort Emerson had described.

The squeak of a floorboard made him tense. He turned his head. God, he hated this. The endless darkness. The constant defensiveness. The soul-shriveling awareness that he was dependent on the sufferance of strangers he couldn't see. He *hated* it!

"Julia?" He wondered fleetingly whether she'd allow herself to be belled like a cat.

"Here, Mr. Williams."

Royce caught the scent of her perfume. At the same time he felt something prod his right hand. He grasped the item. Recognition coincided with the instinctive curling of his fingers. He exhaled in a rush.

"You have to treat this cane like an extension of yourself," Julia reminded him evenly. "*It's* supposed to be taking the knocks, not your shins."

Biting back an obscenity, Royce tightened his grip on the inanimate object he despised as an emblem of his disability. He suddenly recalled a fragment of the conversation he and Julia had had the first time she'd handed him a cane. It had occurred only a few hours after he'd agreed to hire her.

"Haven't you forgotten something?" he'd asked trenchantly, struggling with a furious desire to cast the cane aside. "What about the tin cup?"

He'd heard Julia inhale sharply and known he'd touched a nerve. He'd expected her to get angry. Hell, he'd *hoped* she would! Instead she'd begun to laugh. The soft, rippling sound had triggered a tremor of response deep within his body.

"A tin cup?" she'd echoed with a delicate hint of sarcasm. "No, I don't think so, Mr. Williams. A rich man like you should have something in monogrammed silver. But before you try pulling pity ploys on street corners, you need to master some basic mobility skills. We'll start with the diagonal cane technique...."

Royce drew a steadying breath, then rapped the leg of the chair with the cane. "When did you move this?"

"I didn't. Emerson did."

The response didn't surprise Royce as much as it would have two weeks ago. Although he knew Emerson was loyal to him, he couldn't shake the impression that the older man had formed some kind of alliance with Julia Kendricks in the days since her arrival.

"The chair was *Emerson's* idea?" he questioned after a brief pause.

"Oh, no," Julia immediately denied. "It was mine. He wanted to use something else. Something that would fall over if you walked into it. He suggested one of those Oriental-looking screens in the living room."

Royce was taken aback by this apparently artless disclosure. The lacquered screens in question were antiques. In a house full of expensive objects, they'd been among his father's most prized possessions. Many years ago Royce had accidentally knocked into one of them. Even now, more than three decades after the incident, he could still vividly remember the dressing down Archer Williams had given him for his clumsiness.

"Emerson thought a falling screen would make a bigger impression than a chair," Julia commented with an odd inflection.

"Oh, yes. I'm certain he did," Royce returned tightly.

He knew she must be speculating about his reaction to the older man's "suggestion" about the screen. He wondered briefly whether she'd question him about it, then decided probably not. As intrusive as she was, Julia had shown no inclination toward prying into his private affairs.

Unless...

Unless she'd been soliciting information about him behind his back. From Emerson, for instance.

Royce frowned, forcing himself to consider the implications of this scenario. All right, he thought. Suppose Julia questioned Emerson about the screens. What would he tell her? What *could* he tell her? Exactly how much did he know about the people who'd paid his salary for thirty years?

A lot, Royce admitted after a moment. When it came to the truth about the Williams family, Talley O'Hara Emerson probably knew more than anybody.

Royce forked his free hand back through his hair, uncomfortably conscious that he was venturing into unfamiliar emotional territory. He'd never really stopped to assess how thoroughly Emerson was woven into the fabric of his life. He'd just accepted it.

Emerson had always been there for him, he acknowledged with an odd pang. The older man had never called attention to it, yet he'd always been there when he was needed.

Why?

He was well paid, of course. As a firm believer in the motivational power of money, Royce was confident that this was a crucial part of the answer. Still, he had to confess there were elements of Emerson's behavior he couldn't explain on a strictly bottom-line basis.

There were elements of Julia Kendricks's behavior he couldn't explain on that basis, either. If nothing else, he and Emerson were linked by three decades' worth of shared experiences. But he and Julia? They'd been total strangers until seventeen days ago! Nonetheless, there were moments when Julia acted as though her work with him was some kind of personal crusade.

"Mr. Williams?"

Royce stiffened, trying to orient himself. She'd moved again, damn her. Now she was practically standing next to him. He could smell the feminine fragrance of her flesh, sense the warm temptation of her body. All he had to do was to reach out and he would he able to—

He slammed the brakes on this train of thought. What in the name of heaven was wrong with him? Had he lost his sense of self-preservation along with his sight? Reaching out for Julia Kendricks would be a mistake of monumental proportions. He didn't need twenty-twenty vision to see that!

"Mr. Williams?" Julia repeated.

"What?" Royce snapped. He suddenly felt the stroke of her fingers through the sleeve of his cashmere pullover. The muscles of his belly clenched at the contact. He felt a stirring in his groin.

Was she aware of the effect she had on him? he wondered savagely, shrugging off her touch. Experience had taught him that most women were acutely conscious of the responses they evoked in men. It seemed unlikely that Julia Kendricks was one of the few females who were oblivious to such things. *Highly* unlikely if she was as naturally attractive as Emerson had said she was. Royce had never known a beautiful woman who wasn't fully cognizant of the power of her looks. He'd never known one to shy from taking advantage of that power, either.

And yet something about Julia warned him that it would be unwise to judge her in terms of other women. It went beyond Emerson's comments about her trying to "play down" her looks. Julia Kendricks possessed a quality that made Royce hesitate to classify her as a player of sexual games.

Then why had she...?

A sickening possibility occurred to him.

What if Julia had touched him because she'd felt sorry for him? What if there was *pity* lurking beneath her impudence and sass?

He'd get rid of her, Royce told himself, the fingers of his right hand tightening on his cane. He'd get rid of her in an instant if that were the case, and he'd never think of her again.

Dear Lord, if only he could see her! One look. That's all he'd need to divine the truth about the blond-haired, blue-eyed Miss Kendricks. One long, hard look and he'd know exactly—

"Ahem."

The sound of a throat being cleared came from somewhere off to Royce's left. There was no need for him to ask the identity of the person responsible for it. The noise was as unique as a fingerprint.

"Yes, Emerson?" Royce asked. His awareness of Julia's presence diminished as he did so. He guessed that she'd moved back a step or two.

"There's a call from your secretary, Ms. Hansen," the older man said. "She's on the line in the study."

"Thank you," Royce replied.

"Shall I take you down?"

As offers of assistance went, Royce had to rate this one as extremely tactful. If nothing else, it had been made in a normal tone of voice. Unlike many people, Emerson didn't assume that anyone who was blind had to be hard of hearing, too. Still, the quiet inquiry made Royce's stomach knot. This was his home, dammit! He didn't need help getting around in it!

"That won't be necessary, Emerson," he responded after a moment, struggling to keep his tone polite. He positioned his cane forward, angling it away from his body and holding the tip an inch or so off the floor. Then he turned his head and glared unseeingly toward the spot where he believed Julia was standing. "I'll make it on my own."

You shouldn't have touched him, Julia scolded herself after Royce and Emerson had made their exit from the hallway.

She'd realized the physical contact was a mistake the instant her fingertips had brushed the sleeve of Royce's tobacco brown sweater. His reaction—the sudden rigidity of his posture, the abrupt obliteration of every trace of expression from his compelling face—had made it obvious that he'd interpreted her impulsive gesture of concern as either a show of pity or an act of sexual provocation. Equally obvious: that he was prepared to reject both compassion and come-ons with absolute finality.

He had been wrong in his assessments of her unthinking action, of course. Royce Williams made her feel a great many things, but pity was not one of them.

As for the notion of her trying to tempt him with her feminine wiles . . . no. Dear God, no. *Never.*

Julia sank down on the out-of-place dining room chair. Bowing her head, she buried her face in her palms.

Her mind replayed the image of Royce Williams walking away from her barely a minute before. He'd been using a textbook version of the diagonal cane technique to guide himself. The set of his dark head and broad shoulders had been defiant. His stride had been smooth and sure. Every

inch of his lean, six-foot frame had exuded the message, No
Trespassing.

She'd read the same message in his dark, unseeing eyes
when he'd turned his head toward her and uttered the
words, "I'll make it on my own."

Julia sighed heavily, pressing the heels of her hands
against her cheeks.

Dennis Mitchell had warned her repeatedly that the task
she'd set for herself was an arduous one. Even after she'd
made him understand why it was so desperately important
that she be given a chance to help Royce Williams, the soft-
spoken physician had tried to prepare her for the very real
possibility that she might fail.

"I hope you can get through to him, Julia," he'd said,
studying her from behind the lenses of his wire-rimmed
glasses. "Royce is my best friend. He's also his own worst
enemy. He's in a very dark place, and it's not just because
he's been blinded."

"I'm an expert on dark places, remember?" she'd responded, nodding at the photocopied newspaper clippings
she'd spread out on his desk shortly after being admitted
into his office. She'd believed these clippings argued the
sincerity of her purpose far more effectively than the qual-
ifications listed on her neatly typed résumé. "The man you
call your best friend is the reason I didn't die in my own dark
place. I'll get through to him, Dr. Mitchell. I know I can't
do anything to restore his eyesight. But I swear to you, I'll
find a way to bring some light back into his life."

Julia lowered her hands from her face. "No matter what
it takes, I *will* find a way," she repeated fiercely.

She hadn't been exaggerating when she'd told Dennis
Mitchell she would have been dead if not for Royce Williams. She literally owed her life to the man.

There'd been a time when she would have considered this
a meager debt. A time when she believed her life had little
value and even less meaning. That she'd been blessed with
an opportunity to learn differently was something she owed
to Royce Archer Williams, as well....

* * *

New York City
Ten Years Earlier

It was cold. Bone-piercingly, soul-penetratingly cold. Sixteen-year-old Juline Fischer had heard a TV weathercaster blame the subzero situation on something he'd called the "Arctic Express."

Juline shivered violently, stamping feet that had long since gone numb. The soles of the high-heeled boots she had on were worn very thin. The boots themselves were too tight to accommodate a pair of socks.

She fumbled with the belt of her flimsy raincoat, trying to buckle it. The task wasn't easy. The belt was stiff from the cold and her gloveless fingers were clumsy. She finally gave up and knotted the belt closed.

Juline scanned the nearly deserted street. She'd been on the stroll for more than two hours and hadn't had a single approach. No walk-ups. No drive-bys. No nothing.

Juline shivered again. She could head east, she told herself. But the trouble with moving east was that the girls who peddled there were highly territorial. Their men were connected. Stone-cold killers, some of them. Or so she'd heard. Killers or not, she knew they wouldn't take kindly to her trying to cut into their business.

Bobby had explained the situation to her when she'd started working. That had been months ago. At least, she thought it was months ago. Juline had lost the knack of keeping track of such things.

Whatever the case, she did remember that it had been warm the day Bobby had laid out the facts for her. Warm enough so the idea of parading around in short-shorts and a halter top had seemed almost...natural.

She wasn't a pro and he wasn't a pimp, Bobby had told her. They just needed some money to get them through a rough patch and he was hoping she loved him enough to do her part. Hadn't he been good to her? Hadn't he been there for her when nobody else had given a damn? He wasn't going to turn her out in Times Square or anything like that. All she had to do was hustle a little trade on the fringe of the serious action. That's *all*.

Well, "all" was a total washout tonight, Juline thought, exhaling on a weary sigh. Her breath condensed into a silvery cloud the instant it left her lips. She dimly recalled a time when she would have regarded this as magical. But that time was gone. She didn't believe in magic anymore. Her only creed these days was survival.

Juline crossed her arms in front of her chest and tucked her hands up under her armpits. She shifted her gaze to the all-night coffee shop across from where she was standing. She had a bit of money stashed away, she mused. It wasn't much. Although she liked to think she'd gotten better at looking out for herself, Bobby could almost always tell when she was holding back. Still, what she had saved might be enough to get her off the hook tonight.

She'd have to be careful how she explained the cash to Bobby, of course. He'd been acting kind of scary in recent weeks, swinging from blue-sky highs to scrape-the-bottom lows with little or no warning. Even so, Juline knew he genuinely cared about her. He could be so sweet sometimes. So sweet and so good. All she had to do was to handle things just right...

She crossed the street.

The coffee shop smelled of a lot of things, including rancid grease. But it was warm. Blessedly, blissfully warm. Juline sat down at the counter, selecting a stool as far from the entrance as she could get.

After a few moments a waitress ambled over. She had sallow skin, bad teeth and lusterless eyes. "Whaddya want?" she inquired in a tone of utter indifference as she tossed down a fly-specked menu.

Juline skimmed the laminated sheet swiftly. She'd always been a good reader. She'd been sounding out words before she'd entered kindergarten. Several of her grade school teachers had said she was advanced for her age and suggested she be skipped ahead. Although nothing had ever come of their recommendations, Juline took secret pride in the fact that she'd once been considered "special."

"Um, I'll have a bowl of chili," she decided after a few seconds. Her stomach growled suddenly, as though endorsing her selection. "That comes with crackers, right?"

The waitress shrugged an apparent affirmation and scrawled a notation on her pad. "Anything else?"

Juline's nose started to run. "Coffee," she said, snuffling. "Please."

The waitress frowned at the courtesy, almost as though she was contemplating taking offense at it. Then she shrugged a second time. "Yeah, right," she muttered, and ambled away.

The chili was hot, filling, and a lot tastier than some of the stuff Juline had eaten during her time in New York City. The crackers were stale, but she didn't complain.

"You done yet?" the waitress eventually asked, scratching her scalp with the eraser end of her pencil.

Juline nodded, understanding that the price of a bowl of chili and a cup of coffee didn't entitle her to all-night squatting rights. "Uh-huh," she said. "Can I get my bill?"

"Right here," the waitress replied, producing the check with the first spark of energy she'd shown.

After scrutinizing the woman's math, Juline paid the tab. She left the change she received as a tip.

The night seemed colder than ever. Juline started shivering the instant she stepped out of the coffee shop. Her eyes began to water. The icy air hurt her nostrils and lungs.

She crossed the street, head hunched forward, hands thrust deep into the pockets of her raincoat. As she turned the corner onto a narrow side street, she saw someone step out of the doorway of a boarded-up shop just a few yards ahead. A rush of fear suffused her as she registered the size of the stranger looming before her.

Her breathing pattern broke. Her heart started to hammer.

She opened her mouth to scream, braced herself to turn and run.

"Bobby!" Juline gasped, abruptly realizing who was standing in front of her. She put a shaky hand to her chest. "God, you scared me!"

"Bitch!" Bobby grabbed her roughly and shoved her against the storefront. "What the hell do you think you're doing?"

"W-w-working."

He dismissed this stuttered assertion with a spittle-laced obscenity.

"I w-was," Juline insisted, fighting to keep her voice steady. "Really." She'd never seen Bobby like this. Well, no. That wasn't true. He'd turned junkyard-mean two weeks ago, after he'd gone on a bender with an old buddy. But he hadn't meant to hurt her that night. It had been the drinking and her own behavior that had goaded him to violence. If she hadn't started nagging him, he never would have laid a hand on her. He'd assured her of that when he'd apologized the next morning. And she'd believed him. How could she not, considering the way he'd cuddled her and cried as he'd pleaded for her forgiveness?

"I saw you in that coffee shop, Juline!"

She bit her lower lip. His fingers tightened cruelly on her shoulders. "I had to go to the b-bathroom."

Bobby shook her, knocking the back of her head against the wall. "At the counter?" he demanded. His expression was ugly, his breath sour. There was a feral light in his bloodshot eyes. "On a stool?"

Juline berated herself for having told such a stupid lie. "All right," she confessed, "I—I had a quick c-cup of coffee, too."

Bobby struck her across the face with a brutal, back-handed slap.

"Bobby!" Her invocation of his name came on a shocked exhalation.

He struck her again. Suddenly, Juline was very frightened. Although Bobby had hit her before, he'd always left her face untouched. He'd once said something about not wanting to mark up the merchandise. But now—

Another blow, this one much more punishing than the previous two.

"I'm sorry!" Juline cried, hoping to placate her assailant.

"I'll show you sorry," Bobby snarled. "I sent you out to make money, Juline. Not to spend it!"

"I was hungry, Bobby!" She managed to ward off a slap. "And it got so c-cold—"

"If you'd been hustling the way you're supposed to, you'd've been plenty warm!"

The next punch caught Juline squarely on the bridge of her nose. She experienced a starburst of agony. A moment later she tasted the copper-salt tang of her own blood. She gagged and tried to clear her mouth. Bobby seized a fistful of her hair and yanked her head back.

He hit her again. Her vision blurred. She heard her attacker curse. Then, terrifyingly, she heard him laugh.

That's when Juline Anna Fischer finally started to fight back. Because that's when she accepted the fact that Robert "Bobby" Richards had gone crazy. Crazy enough to kill her if she didn't stop him.

She scratched. She kicked. She bit. She screamed. At least, she thought she screamed. Inside her head the noises she was making certainly sounded like screams.

Screams of rage and pain.

Screams for help and mercy.

Bobby had her down on the pavement. He'd ripped open her raincoat and torn the front of the skimpy nylon dress she had on. He had one knee planted on her chest. His hands were around her throat.

He began to squeeze.

She couldn't...

Tighter. Tighter.

Couldn't...breathe.

And then Juline heard a man yelling. She couldn't make sense of his words. But whatever they were, they caused Bobby to freeze like a wild animal caught in the glare of oncoming headlights.

Juline fainted. How long she was out, she never knew. But when she regained consciousness, Bobby was gone and a stranger was crouched beside her on the sidewalk. He was covering her with something soft and warm.

She tried to say thank you, but she couldn't seem to get her lips or tongue to move. She heard a gurgling moan. After a moment she realized the horrible-sounding noise was coming from her.

"It's all right," the stranger said quickly. He took one of her hands and sandwiched it between his own. "You're safe now. Help is on the way."

Juline tried to speak again. She felt something slimy dribble out of her mouth.

"It's all right," the stranger repeated. His voice was low and soothing, yet firm. Juline thought he sounded as though he was accustomed to having people believe what he said simply because he was the one who said it. "You're going to be okay."

She peered upward, trying to focus on the face that went with the assured, authoritative voice. She wasn't able to see much, but what few details she could make out she imprinted on her heart.

Thick, dark hair.

Long-lashed, deep-set eyes, also dark.

Angular features.

She couldn't tell his age. Maybe thirty. Maybe a few years less than that. There was no hint of boyishness about him.

Juline inhaled on a shuddery breath as a shaft of pain arrowed through her. She squeezed the stranger's long, lean fingers.

"Easy," he counseled. "Easy. They'll be here very soon."

Who's they? Juline wanted to ask. And who...who are *you?*

Her thoughts skittered off in a dozen different directions. There was a weird buzzing inside her ears. Black dots swirled dizzyingly in front of her eyes. Her head started to spin. A brackish taste flooded her tongue.

She must have passed out again. The next thing she knew, she was hearing sirens and seeing flashing lights. At the same time she felt the stranger trying to disengage his fingers from hers. Terror gripped her.

"D-don't," she begged in a broken whisper, clutching at her rescuer with desperate strength. "Please. D-don't... g-go."

"Ahem."

Julia was startled back into the present.

"E-Emerson," she managed, straightening her clothing with shaking fingers as she got to her feet. She registered a fleeting sense of surprise that her legs were steady enough to support her. It had been a long time since she'd gotten so thoroughly trapped in the undertow of memory.

There was a brief silence. Emerson stared at her intently. She stared back, wishing she could figure out what he was thinking.

That Talley O'Hara Emerson was utterly devoted to his employer, Julia had no doubt. She sensed something almost paternal in his attitude toward Royce Williams. Yet there'd been many moments since her arrival when she'd gotten the feeling that Emerson considered himself in cahoots with her. It was as though he understood why she was doing what she was doing and wanted to assist her.

But that was impossible. There was no way Emerson could comprehend her motives without being aware of her true identity. And that was something he simply couldn't be. No one in Boston knew that Julia Kendricks, summa cum laude college graduate with a degree in special education, had once been Juline Anna Fischer, runaway-turned-streetwalker.

No one except for Dennis Mitchell, that is. And he'd been sworn to secrecy. Although Julia did not trust easily or often, she believed Royce Williams's friend and doctor could be taken at his word.

"Royce would like you to join him in the study," Emerson finally announced.

"He would?" Julia echoed dubiously. She found it difficult to imagine that Royce Williams would "like" her to do anything except leave him alone.

The corners of Emerson's mouth crimped as though he'd divined her line of thinking. "I might have exaggerated a bit," he conceded dryly. "Would you believe he didn't kick up too much of a fuss when I said I'd come and get you for him?"

"The operative phrase being 'too much'?"

"Well, he never told me no flat-out."

Julia waited a moment or two, then smoothed a hand down the front of her roomy sweatshirt. Drawing herself up to her full five foot seven, she squared her slim shoulders and stiffened her spine.

"Lead the way, Emerson," she instructed.

"My privilege, Miss Kendricks," the older man responded. "Though I've no doubt you could make it on your own just fine."

Three

"Don't quit now, Mr. Williams. Just eight more."

Grimacing, Royce pulled down on the counterweighted bar of his exercise machine. He brought the bar tight against his chest, holding it until the muscles of his upper arms and back began to quiver in rebellion. He released the bar in a controlled movement, exhaling in an explosive rush.

"That's right."

Royce went through the pull-hold-release sequence again.

"Keep going."

Easy for you to say, he thought as he repeated the exercise. Gritting his teeth, he dragged the bar down yet another time.

The equipment he was using was set up in the dressing area off his bedroom. It had been in storage when Julia had taken up residence under his roof. He'd ordered it packed away after he'd stumbled into it his first night home from the hospital and nearly added a third cracked rib to the pair he'd sustained in his accident.

Precisely how Julia had learned about the exercise gear Royce wasn't sure, although he had a few suspicions. Suffice it to say, her greeting to him on the fourth morning after her arrival had included the information that she'd asked Emerson to have the equipment brought out again. She'd further informed him that Dennis Mitchell had okayed the addition of a workout to their schedule of daily activities.

"Their" schedule, indeed, Royce mocked. Odd, how so many of the activities on "their" schedule involved *her* telling *him* what to do.

He expelled the air from his lungs and released the bar. Then he repeated the exercise. It was a sequence of movements he'd performed countless times during his pre-accident workouts. But the exercise felt different to him this morning.

So many things in his life felt different.

"Six more."

"*Six?*" Julia had attempted to con him into extra repetitions before. Royce knew her real objective was to force him to focus on what he was doing. "Try—" a grunt of exertion "—three."

"Four," she countered immediately. A hint of laughter sparkled in her voice like sunlight dancing on the surface of a breeze-ruffled lake.

He yanked the bar down, held it, then released it.

"Two," he declared flatly.

"Oh, all right," she conceded. "Make it three."

"One." Royce went through the exercise sequence for the final time, then let go of the bar. He experienced a surge of satisfaction as he heard the metallic clank of the machine's weights dropping back into place. "Finished."

Sitting up, he peeled off the cotton T-shirt he had on and began to dry his perspiration-sheened torso. He stretched like a cat, relishing the smooth flex and release of his muscles. As much as he resented Julia's high-handed edict about his exercising, he had to admit he preferred his current condition to the state he'd been in when he'd left the hospital.

A second or two later Royce felt something—a towel, he swiftly determined—drop into his lap.

"Use that, please," Julia requested. The laughter was gone from her voice. She sounded annoyed.

No. More than that, Royce decided after a moment's reflection. She sounded genuinely upset. But why should she be?

He cocked his head, frowning. "Julia?"

"What?"

"Is something wrong?"

There was a brief pause. Then, quietly, "No, Mr. Williams. Everything's fine."

Royce used the towel to blot his arms, stalling as he tried to get a fix on her tone. Analyzing the nuances of pitch and inflection in Julia's expressive voice had become a habit with him during the past two and a half weeks. He thought he'd become pretty adept at interpreting her moods and assessing the meanings that lurked beneath her words. But in this particular instance—

The delicately promising scent of her perfume suddenly teased his nostrils. Royce inhaled involuntarily, conscious of an immediate stiffening in his groin. He felt his exercise-elevated pulse rate scramble.

Not again, he protested silently. Dammit, not again!

Royce had been celibate since his accident. He'd been impotent part of that time—perfectly normal given the circumstances, the so-called experts had assured him. Even after he'd recovered his physical ability to perform, his libido had remained limp. The various specialists who'd poked and prodded him had declared that this was perfectly normal, as well.

Then Dennis Mitchell's musical-voiced protégée had invaded his life and his sex drive had accelerated from full stop to flat-out speeding. She'd aroused him to the point of embarrassment within moments of her arrival!

What the medical community might have to say about this abrupt turn of events, Royce had no idea. Nor did he have any intention of finding out.

He'd never experienced anything as powerful as the erotic response Julia Kendricks evoked in him. Although imbued with the unruly extremity of adolescence, it was intensely, unmistakably adult.

Initially, Royce had tried to ignore his feelings. To downplay their importance. Hell, to dismiss their very existence!

When that had proven impossible, he'd attempted to explain them away.

This tactic had turned out to be worse than unsuccessful.

To put it bluntly, his effort to rationalize the irrational had led to a recognition that he was in danger of becoming obsessed with the fair-haired, blue-green-eyed Ms. Kendricks. Denied the possibility of knowing her by sight, it seemed increasingly vital for him to discover her through his other four senses.

To touch...

To taste...

To hear...

To smell...

To *know* her. Utterly and absolutely.

"Mr. Williams?"

Royce started. She'd moved, he realized instantly. She'd come closer to the exercise machine. A lot closer.

Again, the spring floral fragrance of her skin tantalized him.

"What are you wearing?" he questioned abruptly.

"I beg your pardon?"

"Your perfume," he clarified. He understood it was unwise to ask, unwise to fuel the fascination he felt, but he had to find out.

"My...perfume." Julia sounded surprised. And wary. "It's, uh—"

The name she offered was only vaguely familiar to Royce. It was a name he associated with a brand of reasonably priced toiletries one might find in a drugstore or supermarket.

"Have you worn it long?"

"Why?" The wariness was still there.

"No particular reason." Royce draped the sweat-dampened towel across his thighs, hoping the crotch of his cotton shorts didn't look as tight as it felt. "It—the scent—suits you, that's all."

"Oh." A pause. "I've worn it about a year. It was a present."

Julia's voice softened markedly on the last word. She spoke it tenderly, as though summoning a cherished memory. To Royce, the implication was obvious. It was also astonishingly unpleasant.

"From a lover," he said, not bothering to make it a question.

"What?" she gasped. Then, almost wildly, *"No!"*

There was a jarring, jagged-edged silence.

Talk about fumbling in the dark, Royce thought. He felt as though he'd been dumped into a game of blindman's bluff in the middle of a mine field.

"Look, I didn't mean—" he finally ventured.

"How could you?" Julia interrupted. "How—how could you th-think—?"

"Well, why shouldn't I?" he countered, stung by her accusatory tone. Julia Kendricks was a twenty-six-year-old woman, for heaven's sake! An *attractive* twenty-six-year-old woman, if Emerson's observations and his own masculine instincts were to be trusted. What was so awful about his assuming that she had a lover who gave her gifts? It wasn't as though he'd been implying anything insulting when he'd said—

Or had he?

The possibility stopped Royce cold.

He'd never accepted the idea that there should be one sexual standard for men and another for women. While he was willing to confess to a great many things, subscribing to that type of hypocrisy was not one of them. And yet...

It was different with Julia Kendricks, he admitted to himself with great reluctance. It was different because *she* was different.

Wasn't she?

Certainly, he'd never been aware of another woman the way he was aware of her. Then again, he'd never needed to be. In fact, it had been years—decades, perhaps—since he'd "needed" to be much of anything when it came to dealing with other people. And it had been at least as long since he'd needed them to be much of anything to him.

Royce clenched his hands. Past and present intertwined. Reality turned inward on itself.

Eyes.

Beautiful, blue-green eyes.

He still didn't know why he'd acted as he had on that frigid winter night in New York City. After all this time, he still couldn't explain what had prompted him to succumb to the first and only good Samaritan impulse of his adult life.

Even now he could feel the pressure of the teenager's bloodied fingers. Even now he could hear the pleading of her broken voice.

Don't, she beseeched him. *Please. D-don't . . . g-go.*

He'd had to. He'd given what he had to give, done all he was capable of doing. He'd gone because he'd realized his usefulness was at an end. He'd gone because he'd realized that what the child-woman who'd clung to him with such anguished trustfulness needed was something he simply couldn't provide.

He wanted to believe he'd done the right thing in leaving her. He also wanted to believe that somehow, some way, the girl he'd rescued had come to regard his abrupt departure from her life not as a betrayal of a promise but as a—

Julia's voice, held steady by a palpable effort of will, dammed up this treacherous flood of thoughts.

"The perfume was a birthday present from some of my students," Royce heard her say. "Four girls and five boys, ages nine and ten. I don't have a lover, Mr. Williams. I don't *want* one."

"Julia—"

"You should get changed," she cut in, retreating into cool professionalism. "Let me know when you're ready for your Braille lesson."

Royce reached out for her then, repeating her name in an urgent tone.

The effort was futile. The woman he wanted was gone.

Julia sought refuge in her bedroom. Unfortunately its ivory-and-rose serenity was no match for her stormy state of mind.

"What's happening to me?" she whispered, slumping against the door she'd already closed and locked. That she should feel something special for Royce Williams was to be expected, she tried to assure herself. The man had saved her life. She was grateful to him. And everyone knew gratitude was a very potent emotion.

But was it gratitude she'd felt a few minutes ago when she'd stared at her benefactor's sweat-slicked, suavely muscled torso?

Was it gratitude that had made her knees turn to jelly and her throat go dry in the space of a single pulse beat?

Was it?

No, Julia acknowledged rawly. The responses Royce had aroused in her had little to do with gratitude and even less with the reasons she'd inveigled her way into his life more than ten years after he'd exited from hers.

Even now, she could feel the warmth flickering deep within her. And beneath the warmth, the wanting. The embers of an unfamiliar yearning, banked down but still burning. Banked down, but oh-so-easily stirred back to blazing life.

It's not supposed to be this way, Julia thought, pressing her trembling fingers to her equally unsteady lips. Not now. Not with *him!*

She'd gone through a period after her rescue when she'd had great difficulty allowing anyone to touch her. A platonic pat on the arm had panicked her. The idea of submitting to a kiss had literally made her ill.

Therapy had helped her confront and overcome this revulsion. The members of what had become her surrogate family had done even more. Through countless acts of kindness, they had persuaded her that no matter how filthy she might feel, there were people—clean, decent people—who did not consider her a source of contamination. They had also proven to her that physical contact was not inextricably linked to sexual exploitation or outright abuse.

During the past ten years Julia had progressed from a shame-induced state in which she couldn't accept a handshake without flinching to a point where she was able to initiate a hug without fearing her motives would be misconstrued. This was not to say she offered her embraces impulsively or often. Unless a child was involved, her primary instinct was to withhold herself in every possible way.

A child...or Royce Williams, she amended after a few seconds, slowly lowering her hands from her mouth. The truth was, whatever instincts were shaping her behavior toward the man who'd saved her life, they certainly didn't include one that told her to hold back from him.

She had to come to terms with what she was feeling and the fear it engendered in her. She had no other choice. To fail to do so would be to fail in the task she'd set for herself. And failure was an option she simply couldn't—wouldn't—accept.

She'd waited too long.

She owed him too much.

Julia pushed herself away from the bedroom door. Royce Williams needed her help, and she was going to give it to him. And once she'd given all she could, she would go. But not before then. No matter how difficult the situation became, she wasn't going to—

Knock, knock.

Julia stiffened at the sound, inhaling sharply. She pivoted.

"Miss Kendricks?" The inquiry from the other side of the wooden door was deferential yet determined.

Her posture eased. She released her breath. "Yes, Emerson?"

"Royce asked me to tell you he's ready for his Braille lesson now."

After a fractional hesitation, Julia reached forward and undid the lock. A moment later she turned the knob and opened the door. "What a coincidence," she said, lifting her chin and manufacturing a smile. "I just happen to be ready, too."

"She looks tired," Dennis Mitchell commented late that afternoon.

Royce blinked, his thoughts still focused on the woman who'd just left the room. "What?"

"I said, Julia looks tired."

They were sitting in a pair of leather club chairs that flanked the fireplace in the town house's study. Dennis had arrived on Royce's doorstep about half an hour earlier. He'd claimed his day-after-Christmas visit was an impulsive thing. That he'd happened to be in the neighborhood and decided to drop by.

Royce hadn't challenged this explanation. But given certain geographic facts—namely that his home was in Boston's Back Bay while Dennis lived and worked across the Charles River in Cambridge—he'd harbored a few doubts about its veracity.

At first he'd thought there must be a professional reason for his friend's house call. He'd been forced to abandon this notion after a few minutes of conversation. If Dennis had had something to say about his condition, be it good news or bad, Royce knew he would have said it straight out.

His next thought had been that the visit must be linked to Julia. The longer he'd considered this possibility, the more likely it had seemed. No matter that Dennis had only inquired after her once. There'd been something more than casual disappointment in his voice when he'd been told she was out taking a walk.

And there'd been something more than casual *pleasure* in his voice when he'd greeted her as she'd returned from that walk only minutes later.

"Dr. Mitchell!" Julia had exclaimed. "I didn't realize you were planning to come by today."

Her surprise at Dennis's presence was genuine, Royce had decided. But beneath the surprise, he'd heard uncertainty. Anxiety, even.

"I just happened to be in the neighborhood and decided to drop by," Dennis had responded, repeating the explanation he'd offered previously.

There'd been a brief pause. Royce had sensed an exchange of looks. His chronic resentment of his blindness had spiked like a fever.

After a moment Julia had cleared her throat. "It's good to see you again." She'd sounded as though she were smiling. "Season's greetings."

"Season's greetings to you, too, Julia," Dennis had replied. Royce would have bet money that he had been smiling as well.

Royce gripped the arms of his chair, digging his nails into the smooth leather covering. Something was going on between Julia and Dennis. But without being able to see the two people involved, he was in the dark about exactly what that "something" was.

She looks tired, Dennis had said as soon as she'd left the study, shutting the door behind her.

What the hell was that supposed to mean?

"Royce?"

"I guess I'll just have to take your word about how Julia looks, won't I, Dennis?" Royce said, not making the slightest effort to dull the edge in his voice. "After all, *you* can see her."

"I don't—"

"She looks tired, does she? Why do you suppose that is? Do you think I'm working her too hard? I mean, I didn't even give her Christmas off." Hell, he hadn't even registered that yesterday had been a holiday. As far as he'd been concerned, it had been one more day in the dark. And neither Julia nor Emerson had made any reference to the significance of the date within his hearing.

"Royce—"

Somewhere in the back of his mind Royce realized he was on the verge of saying something inexcusable. He didn't care. Crossing the line into deliberate offensiveness, he gibed, "Or maybe you're worried I'm keeping the lady up at night?"

"Will you please—"

"Why are you so interested in Julia Kendricks, Dennis?" Royce pressed. The urge to lash out was overwhelming. "Tell me that. Just why—"

"Because I feel responsible for her, dammit!" Dennis cut in. "I recommended her to you, remember? I'm one of the reasons she's living under your roof." He sounded angrier than Royce had ever heard him sound, and he seemed to be getting angrier with each word he spoke. "I'm also interested—no, wait, make that concerned. I'm *concerned* about her because I know what you're like, Royce. Even under the best of circumstances, you can be an unmitigated bastard!"

Royce opened his mouth to utter an appropriately anni-
hilating comeback but shut it when he realized that the fury
he'd been experiencing had vanished. In some inexplicable
way, his friend's temper had defused his own.

There was a long silence. Or rather, at least a minute went
by during which neither of them said anything. One of the
things Royce had learned since his accident was that most
"silences" were filled with sounds.

The steady ticking of the clock on the fireplace mantel.

The creaking groan of his club chair as he shifted in his
seat.

The sigh, half apologetic, half exasperated, that told him
Dennis was about to resume speaking.

"I'm sorry, Royce."

Royce made a dismissive gesture. "It's all right."

"No. Really. I shouldn't have—"

"It's all right, Dennis," Royce repeated, meaning it. "I
was way out of line. I appreciate your kicking me back into
it."

There was a short, snorting noise, possibly a smothered
chuckle. "Well, somebody has to do it."

Royce smiled wryly but made no response.

"Does Julia?" Dennis's inquiry was oddly inflected.

"Does Julia what?"

"Kick you back into line when you're out of it."

Royce hesitated for several seconds, then admitted,
"More often than not." He grimaced. "Maybe *that's* why
she looks so tired."

"I wasn't suggesting—"

"Hell, no," Royce interpolated. "You flat-out said I can
be an unmitigated bastard, even under the best of circumstances. And considering that my current circumstances are
anything but..."

There was another pause.

"Has Julia gone out at all since she started living here?"
Dennis eventually asked.

The implied reproach flicked Royce on the raw. "She just
came in from being out a few minutes ago."

"That's not what I meant and you know it."

Royce raked a hand back through his hair. Yes, he knew it. But what in heaven's name was he supposed to say? That except for her daily walks—walks that he was always invited to go along on but always avoided—Julia never left his house? That she seemed bent on making herself available to him virtually twenty-four hours a day?

He hadn't asked for such single-minded devotion, dammit!

"I employ Julia Kendricks, Dennis," he said flatly. "I don't own her. She's free to leave anytime she wants."

"But she won't."

Royce frowned at his friend's tone. It hinted at hidden agendas and closely guarded secrets. "What's that supposed to mean?"

No answer.

"Dennis?" Royce probed.

"This job is important to Julia," Dennis finally said. A series of noises suggested he was shifting—or was it squirming—in his seat. "She's not going to leave until it's finished."

"She'll leave when I get my sight back," Royce countered. He waited a beat, then added, "And I *am* going to get my sight back."

It was intended to be a statement of fact. But even as he uttered the confident-sounding words, Royce knew they held an unspoken plea for reassurance.

"Royce, we've already gone through this."

Royce slammed his right palm against the leather arm of his club chair. "And we'll keep going through it until I get a straight answer!"

"Don't you think I wish I had one to give you?" Dennis demanded. "Don't you think I wish the tests you've undergone had turned up something conclusive? The truth is, I don't know why you've lost your sight. *Nobody* knows. And nobody knows when—or if—it's going to return."

Royce struggled for control. He was angrier at himself than at Dennis. After all, he'd asked for it. Now all he had to do was figure out how to endure it.

His mind flashed back to his first meeting with Julia.

Do you honestly believe you can teach me to accept being blind? he'd asked.

No, she'd answered. *Acceptance is a lesson you have to learn on your own, Mr. Williams.*

"In other words, you may have recommended Julia for a permanent position."

Dennis exhaled heavily. "I sincerely hope not."

The question, "For whose sake?" teetered on the tip of Royce's tongue but he swallowed it. Finally he brought their conversation full circle. "Do you really think she looks tired?" he asked.

"Yes." A pause. Then, slowly, "What would you say to my inviting her to dinner tonight?"

So much for the just-happened-to-be-in-the-neighborhood ploy, Royce thought sardonically. He should have known. Oh, hell, he *had* known. He'd known the first time he'd heard Dennis say Julia's name.

Well, Dennis was welcome to her. *He* certainly didn't want her. Or need her. At least, not in any meaningful way. To lust after a woman he couldn't see wasn't meaningful. It was—

Never mind what it is! Royce told himself.

"What would I say to your inviting Julia to dinner tonight?" he echoed, turning his head toward his friend. "I'd say you're asking the wrong person."

Four

—

"**So?**" Dennis Mitchell prompted after the waiter who'd brought their appetizers bustled away. "How are things going with Royce?"

Julia picked up her fork and speared a sun-dried tomato from the half portion of pasta she'd ordered. "As compared to what?"

Dennis's brows chased after his receding hairline. "That bad?"

Julia conveyed the tomato to her mouth, chewed and swallowed. She gazed across the table at her dinner companion, speculating about the friendship between him and Royce Williams. It wasn't the first time she'd done so. They were such very different men. Where Royce was dark, lean, and dangerously compelling, Dennis was fair-haired, a few pounds overweight, and merely pleasant-looking. Where Royce was more complicated than a Chinese puzzle box, Dennis was refreshingly straightforward. And where Royce was capable of rousing her to a fever pitch...

"You warned me this would be difficult," she conceded, forking up a small tangle of fettuccine.

"Yes, well...I hope I haven't made the situation worse."

The pasta landed back on Julia's plate with a soft plop. "Worse?"

"I don't think Royce was very pleased about your going out with me this evening."

Julia set down her fork, conscious of a sudden tightening in her chest. "I had the distinct impression he couldn't wait to get rid of me."

An odd expression flickered through Dennis's eyes. "Is *that* why you finally accepted my dinner invitation?"

Julia glanced away, trying to mask her agitation. Had Dennis issued his invitation to her in private, she almost certainly would have turned him down. Unfortunately he'd asked her out to dinner in Royce's presence. Royce's immediate seconding of the idea had made it virtually impossible for her to say no. Which wasn't to say she hadn't tried. She had. Repeatedly. But every excuse she'd offered had been ruthlessly rejected. And not by Dennis. By Royce.

"You're entitled to some time off," he'd declared after she'd run through a laundry list of reasons why she couldn't have dinner with Dennis. She'd even been driven to mouthing a hopelessly hokey line about not having anything appropriate to wear. Unfortunately, Dennis had responded to her demurral with some complimentary assurances about her appearance. Royce had dismissed it with a quick, curt gesture.

"Mr. Williams—" she'd started to protest.

"I don't need you here tonight, Julia," he'd interrupted. His tone had strongly implied he didn't *want* her there, either.

A moment later she'd succumbed to the inevitable and accepted Dennis's invitation.

Julia looked back at the man who'd once described Royce Williams as his best friend. "Dr. Mitchell—"

"Dennis," he corrected. "Please. Call me Dennis."

"Dennis," she repeated after a second or two. "Look. I don't want you to think... I mean... my coming to dinner with you tonight—"

He smiled as she made an awkward gesture and lapsed into an even more awkward silence. "It's all right, Julia," he assured her. "I understand."

"You do?"

He nodded. "And *you* have to understand that Royce doesn't always mean what he says—or say what he means."

It took Julia a few moments to digest the implications of this assertion. "You *honestly* believe he didn't want me to go out with you?"

"He probably convinced himself he did," Dennis replied, picking up his wineglass. He eyed her over the rim. "But deep down..."

There was a long pause.

"You've known Royce a long time, haven't you," she finally ventured.

"It's been—" Dennis seemed to calculate the length of time in his head "—more than twenty years. We roomed together in prep school. I was a geeky scholarship kid who'd never been away from home. Royce was an all-around athlete with a multimillion dollar trust fund whose father shipped him off to boarding school when he was eight."

Something about the phrasing of the last sentence struck Julia as peculiar. It took her a moment to sort out what it was.

"What about his mother?" she questioned.

"I don't think she had much say in the matter."

Julia mulled this over, remembering the lovely silver-framed photograph on the desk in Royce's study. If there were any pictures of his father in the town house, she hadn't seen them.

"They were close, weren't they?" she asked after a few seconds. "Royce and his mother, I mean." She had trouble saying Royce's name aloud. Although she'd thought of him that way for many years, abandoning the formal "Mr. Williams" she always used when speaking about him seemed risky.

"Very," Dennis answered. "Royce adored his mother. And Margaret—that was her name, Margaret—adored him. But the relationship didn't sit well with Royce's father. He—Archer—was a lot older than Margaret. I suppose he was jealous of her giving her time or attention to anyone but him. And even though he wanted a son to carry on the family legacy, he basically viewed Royce as a piece of property, not a person.''

"What happened to her? I know she died.''

"It was near the end of our sophomore year at prep school. She took very sick, very suddenly. She died less than forty-eight hours after she was hospitalized. If Emerson hadn't phoned—''

"Emerson?"

"Well, actually, I'm not positive about that,'' Dennis conceded. "I've always assumed it must have been Emerson. All I know for certain is that Royce and I were in our room studying for exams when somebody yelled that he had a call on the house phone. He went and took it. When he came back he told me he'd just found out his mother was dying and he was leaving to be with her.''

"Couldn't it have been his father who called?''

Dennis shook his head, his expression grim. "If Archer Williams had wanted Royce to come home, he would have phoned the headmaster. Royce left campus without permission and hitchhiked back to Boston.''

"Did he get to see his mother before—?''

"He's always been pretty tight-lipped about exactly what happened. But I know he was with her at the end. I also know his father went into a rage when Royce showed up at the hospital. *That's* when Archer Williams called the school. He apparently raised holy hell about Royce's sneaking away.''

Julia bit her lip. Although she was no stranger to cruelty, this story shocked her.

"Given the clout Archer had with the board of trustees—the Williams's name is on two school buildings—the headmaster couldn't really argue back,'' Dennis went on. "Besides, rules were rules. Royce should have been expelled for what he did, but all he got was a lecture and a couple hours of detention. Plus, the headmaster arranged for him to take part in a special travel program so he didn't have to go home for the summer. Royce came into a chunk of money when he graduated. He moved out of the town house at that point. I don't think he saw Archer more than half a dozen times in the next six years. Archer died of a massive stroke when Royce was twenty-four. Royce told me later the only reason he went to the funeral was to make sure the son of a bitch was really gone.''

They moved on to more pleasant subjects after that. Dennis proved to be an amiable dinner partner. Julia found herself growing increasingly comfortable with him as the evening wore on. The energy between them was very different from the volatile give-and-take that characterized her relationship with Royce Archer Williams.

It was only as they lingered over dessert and coffee that she detected a change in Dennis's demeanor. His bantering conversation began to sound a bit forced. The expression in his eyes took on an odd, assessing quality as he gazed across the table at her.

Julia was accustomed to having men look at her. Well, no, ''accustomed'' wasn't the right word. She would never become accustomed to the hot, hungry stares she sometimes received. But she *had* come to terms with the fact that she'd been endowed with a face and figure that excited masculine attention. She didn't particularly like it. Indeed, she didn't really understand it. The woman she saw when she looked in a mirror didn't seem beautiful or desirable. Still, she'd learned to deal with the reality that many men considered her both.

''What?'' she finally asked Dennis.

''What...what?''

''You've been staring at me.''

Dennis flushed. ''I'm sorry. I wasn't trying to, uh...it's just that, well, I'm having a hard time reconciling Julia Kendricks with, uh, uh...''

''A half-dead teenage whore named Juline Fischer?''

A grimace. ''That's a very ugly way of putting it.''

''Prostitution is a very ugly way of life.''

''I realize that.'' The color in Dennis's face was still much higher than normal. ''Which makes it all the more difficult for me to, I mean, how in heaven's name did you wind up—'' He broke off, plainly appalled at his own inquisitiveness. ''I apologize, Julia. I have no right to ask you that.''

"Considering the risk you took when you recommended me to Royce, I think you have a right to ask just about anything you want," Julia returned evenly. "I don't mind talking about my past. It's mine. I can't deny it. I *should* have told you everything the day I came to your office. I would have, if you'd asked."

There was a pause.

"Only if you're absolutely sure you want to," Dennis finally said.

Julia drew a steadying breath, giving herself a few seconds to organize her thoughts.

"My father died in a construction accident when I was ten," she began. "He was a good man. Hard-working. Kind. My mother...well, she went to pieces when he was killed. She had a problem being alone. So she went out looking for company. For someone to take care of her, really. A couple of weeks after my fourteenth birthday, she got married to a man named Wesley Summers."

Julia averted her gaze then, struggling against an all-too-familiar rush of revulsion.

"Julia?"

The invocation of her name was quiet but compelling. After a few moments she forced herself to face the man sitting across from her and continue with her story.

"Things were okay at first," she said. "Wesley didn't pay much attention to me. And my mother seemed happy. Then, after about a year, Wesley got fired from his job. He started drinking. And once he had a few drinks in him, he got...mean."

"He hit you?"

Julia nodded, plucking at the sleeve of the pullover sweater she was wearing. She reminded herself that the events she was recounting were over and done with. The past couldn't hurt her unless she allowed it to.

"Eventually Wesley's unemployment ran out," she said, picking up the thread of her narrative. "There was no money coming in. My mother went to work as a hostess on the night shift at a local restaurant. About the same time, I started...changing. I'd always been one of the tallest girls in my class. And one of the skinniest. But in the middle of my sophomore year I, um, I—uh ..."

"Matured."

"Yes." The shadowed grimness she saw in Dennis's eyes told her he'd deduced where her story was heading. "At first, all Wesley did was look. Then he began touching me. I tried to ignore it. When that didn't work, I slapped his hands and told him he'd better keep them to himself. He laughed and said any girl who looked the way I did was going to have to get used to having a man's hands on her. Still, he backed off. For a while. Then one night, while my mother was at work ... he came into my bedroom."

Julia lowered her gaze and clenched her fingers, willing herself to go on. "He was too drunk to do anything. And the next morning he acted like he didn't remember, so I decided to keep quiet. About ten days later he came into my room again. He wasn't so drunk this time. I managed to fight him off. I told him I was going to tell my mother. He said she'd never believe me. And he was right. My mother slapped me across the face when I told her what he'd tried to do. She slapped me...and she said I was a lying little bitch who wanted to wreck her marriage."

Dennis made an inarticulate sound of protest.

"Two nights later Wesley came into my room again. And that time—" Julia swallowed convulsively "—I let him d-do what he w-wanted."

"You were *fifteen* years old!" Dennis's voice was soft but full of fury. "For God's sake, Julia! Don't blame yourself for what that perverted bastard did."

Julia looked across the table, stunned, and more than a little moved, by the depth of his outrage. It still astonished her when people got angry *for* her, rather than at her.

"I don't," she answered simply. "I used to. But I don't anymore."

Dennis studied her silently for several seconds. "Wasn't there *anyone* you could turn to for help?"

"My own mother didn't believe me when I told her," she reminded him. "Why should anyone else? Besides, I was afraid. And ashamed. I tried to pretend it was happening to someone else. I'd make my body go numb and my mind go blank. But I wasn't strong enough to keep it up. I started thinking about killing myself. Or Wesley. Finally, I stole some money out of my mother's purse and ran away."

"To New York?"

"Yes." Julia sighed. "You've read the newspaper articles. What happened to me isn't a very original story. Except for the ending. Instead of winding up dead in a gutter, I got a second chance." She hesitated for a moment, then asked, "Has Royce ever talked to you about what he did for me?"

"No. Not really." The reply was reluctant, as though Dennis feared it might hurt her. "Given who he is, the story of his rescuing you got a fair amount of coverage in the Boston papers. I'll admit I was curious about what I read. But Royce shut me down, hard, whenever I tried to bring up the subject. Eventually, I pretty much put the whole episode out of my mind."

Julia absorbed this information in silence. What, if anything, had saving her meant to Royce Williams? she wondered. Had the memory of what he'd done stayed with him? Had he ever speculated about what might have become of the girl he'd—

Julia suddenly realized Dennis had resumed speaking.

"W-what?" she stammered.

"I asked you if it bothers you," he replied. "The fact that Royce hasn't talked about what happened."

"Oh." She shook her head. "Oh, no. Of course not."

Dennis opened his mouth as if to challenge that, then apparently changed his mind and shut it again. After several seconds of silence he asked, "What happened to the man Royce saved you from?"

"He died that same night. The police told me he'd overdosed."

Her dinner companion muttered something that might have been "good riddance."

"I wasn't sure how to feel when I heard," Julia confessed. "I hated Bobby for hurting me. But I couldn't help remembering the good times we'd had together. Finding out he was dead was, well, the first thing I thought when the police told me was that I was alone again. Totally alone."

"What about your..." a slight hesitation "...mother?"

"The police used some identification they found in my bag to track her down." Julia shrugged, feigning indifference. "She told them as far as she was concerned, she didn't have a daughter."

"Dear Lord."

"I wouldn't have gone back." The words came out in a rush, overwhelming her efforts to pretend she hadn't been desperately hurt by her mother's rejection. "Even if she'd said she'd wanted me to, I *never* would have gone back."

"Of course not," Dennis concurred. Then he frowned. "But you were still a minor. The authorities wouldn't have allowed you to waltz out of the hospital on your own."

"They wouldn't let me limp out, either," Julia said wryly, trying to regain her emotional equilibrium. "Once I was discharged, I was placed with a foster family named Kendricks. John and Emily Kendricks. They have three sons. Two by adoption, Ty and Lee—they were both seven. And one biological son, Peter. He was five. He was born blind."

"Ah." There was a wealth of comprehension in the single syllable.

"I probably would've run away the first night if it hadn't been for Peter," Julia admitted frankly. "I figured Emily and John had to be setting me up for something twisted. I mean, I couldn't believe they were as nice as they seemed. Then there was this problem with my scaring Ty and Lee. Bobby did a lot of damage to my face when he beat me. Nothing irreparable. Still, I was bruised and swollen and...ugly...when I left the hospital. Ty and Lee thought I was some kind of freak." She blinked against a sudden threat of tears, remembering how the two boys had shied away from her. "But when it came time for Peter to go to bed that first night, he asked me if I'd read him a story. He said I had a pretty voice."

"You do," came the quiet affirmation. "And no matter what you might have looked like ten years ago, you're anything but ugly now."

Unnerved by this unexpected compliment, Julia shifted in her seat. "At least I don't frighten little kids anymore."

Dennis furrowed his brow, obviously troubled by her reply. For a moment Julia thought he might call her on it. Instead he gently prompted her to go on with her recitation.

"Royce Williams saved my life," she told him, thankful he hadn't pursued the issue of her looks. As empathetic as Dennis Mitchell was, Julia knew he'd never understand the intensely contradictory feelings her appearance aroused in her. "The Kendricks showed me what I could do with it. Peter was the one who started calling me Julia. Pretty soon, everybody in the family was doing it. And since I didn't have any real attachment to Juline..." She gestured. "When I turned eighteen, the foster care system cut me loose. The Kendricks could have done the same. Instead they told me I was welcome to stay with them if I wanted to." She smiled crookedly. "*If* I wanted to!"

Dennis smiled back at her. "I take it you did."

"More than anything in the world," she replied. "I finished high school and won a scholarship to college. I majored in special education. When I turned twenty-one, I asked John and Emily whether they'd mind if I legally changed my last name to theirs. They said they'd be honored. The day the paperwork was signed and notarized, Ty, Lee and Peter presented me with a certificate announcing that they'd taken a vote, and I was officially declared their sister." Julia paused, feeling her eyes grow moist. "And that, Dr. Mitchell, is how Juline Fischer became Julia Kendricks."

Five

"What do the Kendricks think about what you're doing here in Boston?" Dennis asked.

It was shortly before midnight. They were driving along Massachusetts Avenue, heading toward the Charles River Basin. They'd left the restaurant about five minutes ago, following a brief dispute over the check. Despite Dennis's protests that she was his guest for the evening, Julia had insisted on paying her share of the bill. She *always* insisted on paying her share. It was one of the ways she had of emphasizing to herself that she could no longer be bought—by anyone, for any price, for any purpose.

"They understand," Julia answered. Her reply was honest, to a point. While her surrogate family understood the obligation she felt to Royce Williams, she knew they harbored some reservations about her method of discharging it.

Dennis braked for a red light. Glancing to his right, he commented in a reflective tone, "To wait more than ten years..."

"The amount of time isn't important, Dennis." Julia sighed heavily. "I used to daydream about how I'd repay

Royce. What I never considered was that all my fantasies hinged on something awful happening to him."

"You never saw Royce, never contacted him, after that night in New York?"

"I was pretty out of it for the first few days I was in the hospital. By the time my brain started to clear, he was gone. I asked a lot of questions about him, but no one wanted to talk. I finally got his name—Royce Archer Williams—from one of the orderlies. The same orderly told me everyone was buzzing about the fact that this Mr. Williams had arranged to pay my medical bills. He also showed me some newspaper stories about what had happened. That's when I began to feel grateful Royce hadn't stuck around."

"What do you mean?" The light changed to green and Dennis transferred his foot from the brake to the gas.

"The headline in one of the tabloids was 'Harvard Blueblood Saves Battered Hooker.' A pretty succinct summation, don't you think? Not that I needed to have my nose rubbed in the differences between the two of us."

"Royce isn't a snob, Julia." The assertion was sharp. "If he were, he and I never would've become friends. He wouldn't have cared—"

"Maybe not," Julia cut in. "But I did."

They drove along in silence for a few more minutes. As they turned onto Commonwealth Avenue, Dennis picked up the thread of their conversation.

"What about later?" he probed. "If Juline Fischer didn't want to get in touch with the man who'd saved her life, what about Julia Kendricks? You said you'd kept track of Royce through newspapers and magazines. You could have called Williams Venture."

"And then what? Tried to explain to his secretary why I needed to speak with her boss?" Julia mimed putting a telephone to her ear and infused her next words with an artificial perkiness. "Hello, I'm Julia Kendricks. A few years back, when I was a teenage prostitute named Juline Fischer, Mr. Williams saved me from being beaten to death by my drug-crazed pimp. Do you think he might have a couple of minutes to chat?"

"Julia—"

"And supposing the secretary had put me through?" she went on, abandoning the affected voice. "What could I have said to him, Dennis? *What in the name of heaven could I have said?*"

There was a brief pause. Then Royce Williams's best friend softly suggested, "What about 'thank you'?"

Julia averted her head. She inhaled on a shudder. "That wouldn't have been enough," she murmured. "Not then. Not now. Not ever."

Dennis brought his car to a halt in front of Royce's four-story town house a short time later. Except for the copper-and-glass lamps that flanked the front door, the place was dark.

"Looks like everyone's asleep," Dennis observed, turning off the engine and setting the parking brake. "Are you going to be able to get in?"

"I've got a key," Julia said, undoing her seat belt.

"Good." A snick marked the release of his own safety harness.

Dennis got out of the car, letting in a frigid gust of night air. Slamming the door, he walked around to where Julia was sitting.

"Have you decided how long you're going to stay with Royce?" he asked as he handed her out.

He'd questioned her about this the day she'd come to his office to plead for his help. She repeated a variation of the answer she'd given him then. "I'll stay as long as there's something I can do for him."

Dennis shut the car door. "What if his blindness is permanent?"

Julia felt her heart skip a beat. A shiver that had nothing to do with the cold ran through her. *"What do you know?"* she demanded tensely.

"Nothing." Dennis's reply was quick and unequivocal. "We still don't have a definite fix on what's caused Royce's loss of sight, or if there's a treatment for it."

"Then why did you ask—?"

"Because I'm concerned. For both of you."

Julia wasn't certain how to respond to this, so she refrained from saying anything while they crossed the small distance from the car to the town house. Once at the door, she opened her purse and began hunting around inside it.

"Julia—" Dennis started as she fished out her door key and inserted it in the lock.

She looked up at him, hearing anxiety in his voice. "It's all right, Dennis," she said. "I know what I'm doing. And why I'm doing it. As soon as Royce's vision returns, I'm gone. And if it doesn't...well, there'll come a time when I'll have done all I can for him. That's when I'll leave."

"Without telling him the truth."

"Yes." Julia studied Dennis's expression with a sudden surge of uneasiness. "You promised you wouldn't say anything."

"I realize that."

"But?" she prodded. She didn't want Royce to know the truth. It would serve no purpose. She had reentered his life as Julia Kendricks and she intended to exit it the same way. How he remembered her once she did would have nothing to do with how he remembered Juline Fischer... *if* he remembered her at all.

"But nothing," Dennis replied. "I promised I wouldn't say anything and I won't."

Julia searched his face for signs of deceit. She didn't find any. Finally she said, "Thank you."

"You're welcome."

She turned the key and pushed open the front door. Pausing before she stepped inside, she looked at her companion once again and smiled. "I had a lovely time tonight, Dennis."

Dennis, Royce repeated silently, gripping the frame of the study door. *When it's just the two of them, she calls him* Dennis.

Julia's efforts to refuse Dennis's dinner invitation hadn't fooled Royce. He'd known she'd wanted to accept. Any doubts he might have had about this had dissolved when he'd heard her hackneyed protest about not having anything to wear. She'd been fishing for compliments—the kind of compliments a blind man couldn't offer. No matter.

Dennis, nearsighted though he might be, had been ready, willing and able to provide them.

Heaven only knew what else Julia had wanted this evening. And heaven only knew how much of it her dinner companion—*his best friend*—had supplied. But given the length of time they'd been gone...

They'd left about seven. Royce knew this because the clock in the study had chimed seven times several minutes before he'd heard Dennis's car drive away from the front of his town house. It was now shortly past midnight. The same clock had chimed twelve times just moments ago.

He'd been in his study all evening. Doing what, he really couldn't say. He vaguely remembered having listened to an audiotape of an investment prospectus his staff had had couriered over that morning.

Emerson, usually a great respecter of his privacy, had invaded his sanctuary at least a half dozen times. Realizing he was on the verge of losing his temper because of the repeated intrusions, Royce had finally told the older man to take the rest of the night off. Emerson had promptly retreated upstairs. Whether he'd subsequently retired for the evening was a question mark.

Royce heard the front door close. A thunk told him Julia had thrown the bolt. A metallic scraping indicated she'd put on the chain, as well.

A rustle of material.

The tap-tap of shoe heels against the entrance hall's hardwood floor.

Then, finally, the click of the foyer light switch being turned on.

Royce knew to the instant when Julia realized he was standing in the doorway of the study. A swift inhalation of breath betrayed her.

"Julia," he said calmly, envisioning a sudden rush of color to her cheeks or the fluttering lift of a hand to her breast. He began to walk forward.

"I—I thought you'd gone to b-bed," she stammered.

Royce came to a halt, conscious that he'd moved to within touching distance. Julia's voice made it easy to orient himself.

"What made you think that?" he inquired.

"The house was dark."

"Really?" He lifted his brows. "I hadn't noticed."

"I—"

"Did you have a pleasant evening?"

"Uh, yes." She cleared her throat. "Yes. Very pleasant."

"And *Dennis?*" Royce stressed the name, wanting Julia to understand her smoke screen of formality hadn't deceived him. "Did he have a very pleasant evening, too?"

"I—I hope so."

He could hear the nervousness in her voice. Sense the tension in her body. She was off balance. Unsettled. And he was glad of it.

"What did you finally decide to wear?" he asked after a moment.

"Wear?"

"You claimed you didn't have anything appropriate to wear out to dinner, remember? But after you accepted *Dennis's*—" again, the emphasis "—invitation, you went upstairs to change. I wondered what you'd put on."

"Oh." He had the odd impression that Julia had to glance down at herself to determine how to answer him. "Just a black skirt and sweater."

"And high heels."

"Uh, well, yes." She sounded startled. "But how did you—?"

"I heard them."

"I see."

"I don't," he retorted, his grip on his temper starting to weaken. "Which is why I think you should wear heels all the time, not just when you go out with other men. I'm sick and tired of those damn sneakers you put on when you're around me. I can't keep track of you."

"I didn't realize—"

Goaded, he snapped, "Didn't you?"

An unsteady intake of breath. An even shakier exhalation. Then, carefully, "No, I didn't, Mr. Williams."

Her use of his last name was deliberate. There was no question about that. Royce could sense Julia summoning up the professional persona she'd employed so effectively since her arrival. She was distancing herself from him emotionally. Any second now, she'd start distancing herself physically, as well.

No, he thought. I'm not going to let that happen. Not tonight.

Reaching out with his right hand, Royce sought and found Julia's face. She trembled in the first instant of contact but didn't turn away. He felt a surge of triumph.

He mapped the contours of her left cheek with infinite care, testing how far her tolerance of his touch would extend. Clichéd phrases—velvet-soft, satin-smooth—sleeted through his brain. None of them adequately described the exquisite texture of Julia Kendricks's skin.

Emboldened, Royce lifted his left hand and cupped the right side of her face. Again, he felt her tremble. Again, she didn't turn away.

He began to explore Julia's features.

The curve of her forehead.

The arch of her brows.

The length and thickness of her lashes.

Fantasy images gave way to firm-fleshed reality.

Yes, Royce thought. Oh, yes. At long last, he could *see* her in his mind's eye.

Except for an odd quirk at the bridge, Julia's nose was beautifully molded. Her cheekbones were high-set. Her jaw, elegantly defined.

And her mouth.

Dear God in heaven. Her mouth!

The lushness of Julia Kendricks's lower lip was seductive in the extreme. Royce charted its tempting shape with the pads of his thumbs. He was momentarily puzzled by a hint of slickness he picked up. Then he realized what he was feeling.

Makeup.

Julia had done more than change her clothes for the man who'd given her such a glowing job endorsement. She'd put on makeup, as well.

"Please." He suddenly heard her whisper. Her warm breath misted his knuckles. "Oh, please..."

She wasn't asking him to stop. Royce was absolutely certain of that. But neither was she urging him to go on. In fact, he had the strangest sense she wasn't really speaking to him. It was as though she were engaged in an inner struggle and she was pleading with herself.

A moment later he felt her fingers curl up and over his wrists. A tremor of response rocked him from head to heel.

Royce tried to tell himself later that he never would have done what he did next if Julia hadn't touched him. But it wouldn't wash. Because he knew that what he did next was something he'd wanted to do the first time he'd heard her voice.

He kissed her.

He intended only to taste. To tease. To take a few seconds' worth of pleasure. But those intentions went up in flames the white-hot instant his mouth claimed hers.

Julia's lips were stiff and sealed at first. Then, without warning, without any coaxing from him, they grew pliant. They parted like the petals of an exotic flower.

Her hands glided from his wrists, to his upper arms, and finally came to rest on his shoulders. Royce felt the clutch of her palms followed by the bite of her nails through the fabric of his shirt.

He slid his own hands back, splayed fingers spasming possessively in the silken abundance of her hair. The coiffure Julia had devised for her evening with Dennis—some sort of smooth coil at the nape of her slender neck—came apart in a cascade of curls and bobby pins.

Royce lifted his mouth a fraction of an inch. Using the tip of his tongue, he charted the budding curve of Julia's upper lip and the ripened fullness of her lower one. He wondered fleetingly exactly what color her mouth was. Then, tilting her head to the right and his own to the left, he deepened the caress.

Julia's response to him was as arousing as anything he'd ever known. Yet there was a strange element of awkwardness—of uncertainty, even—about the way she kissed.

I don't have a lover, she'd insisted less than twenty-four hours ago.

Lord, was it possible—?

Suddenly the body that had been arching against his with such alluring sweetness went rigid. Stunned by the abrupt change, Royce broke the kiss and eased back a little.

"Royce, stop—" Julia entreated in a breathless voice. He felt the press of her palms against his chest.

He opened his mouth to ask her what was wrong but never uttered the question. He didn't need to.

The raspy rumble of a throat being carefully cleared explained just about everything.

Six

"**O**ne soft-boiled egg, directly in front of you," Emerson was informing Royce as Julia entered the dining room the following morning. "Two slices of buttered toast, above your fork. There's jam to the left. Strawberry. Orange juice next to— Ah, Miss Kendricks. Good morning."

"Good morning, Emerson," Julia said, lifting her chin slightly and willing herself to meet the older man's gaze without flinching. "I'm sorry I'm late. I, uh, forgot to set my alarm clock."

The last sentence was not quite accurate. What Julia had actually forgotten to do was to *re*set her clock. It had gone off as usual, at 6:30 a.m., yanking her out of what had been a singularly restless slumber. After smacking the shrilling alarm into silence, she'd rolled over, burrowed her face into her pillow and gone back to sleep.

She'd awoken with a start about an hour later, her body telling her brain things about the dream she'd been having she would have preferred not to know. Less than ten minutes after that she'd been showered, dressed and dashing down the stairs to the dining room.

"No need to explain," Emerson responded pleasantly. "Will you be having your usual breakfast?"

Julia's stomach churned at the thought of food but she forced herself to ignore the rebellion. If Emerson had the brass to behave as though everything was hunky-dory normal, so did she.

Unable to stop herself, Julia glanced at Royce. She watched him reach forward with his right hand and locate the glass of orange juice Emerson had spoken of a few moments before. A jitter of reaction ran through her as his lean fingers curved around the glass in a slow almost sensuous movement. The jitter became a jolt as he lifted the glass and drank deeply from it.

His mouth, she thought, remembering.

Oh, Lord. His mouth!

The satin-skinned firmness of his lips.

The arousingly evocative search of his tongue.

What had happened in the foyer less than eight hours ago had been the most intensely intimate act Julia Kendricks had ever experienced. For all that her body had gone through, there was a part of her that had always remained untouched. Unawakened. Almost virginal.

Then Royce Archer Williams had kissed her.

And she, heaven help her, had kissed him back.

Julia had been afraid of Royce in the first few seconds after she'd turned around and seen him standing in the doorway of his darkened study. She'd sensed an aura of anger about him and had instinctively prepared herself to flee or fight or both. Her readiness to repay the debt she owed did not include a readiness to return to the role of victim.

But the fear and all that went with it had dissolved in a surge of pleasure the instant Royce had reached out and stroked his fingertips against her cheek. She'd known with absolute certainty that the man who was touching her would never do her any physical harm.

Her knees had nearly buckled when Royce had been exploring her face. His hands had been so gentle. So cherishing. Never in her life had she received such tenderness from a man. From an unfledged little boy of five, yes. But never from a fully grown man.

Julia had felt renewed by his touch. Reborn. It had been as though the very essence of who and what she was was finally being—

"Miss Kendricks?" Emerson's polite voice stemmed the flow of her thoughts.

Julia looked at the older man. He looked back, his expression bland to the point of blankness.

"The usual will be fine, Emerson," she said after a moment. She was surprised by how steady her voice was. Her pulse was anything but. "Thanks."

Emerson nodded, then turned his head. "Anything more for you, Royce?"

Royce placed the now-empty juice glass back on the linen-draped table. "Nothing, Emerson. Thank you."

The older man exited through the swinging wooden door that led from the dining room to the kitchen. At the same time Julia moved around the table and seated herself to Royce's right. A place had already been laid for her. She unfolded the napkin provided and draped it across her lap.

Then she waited. For precisely what, she wasn't certain. But it definitely was for something more than Emerson's return with her "usual" breakfast of yogurt-topped fruit and tea.

A minute or so ticked away. Julia finally slanted an uneasy look at Royce. The lines bracketing his mobile mouth seemed deeper than usual. There were shadowy smudges beneath his eyes, too. It appeared that she hadn't been the only one who'd had trouble sleeping the night before.

Royce picked up the knife to the right of his plate and used his left hand to locate the eggcup sitting in front of him. His movements were careful but confident, a testament to how far he'd come in coping with the challenges posed by his sightless state.

Julia had helped him, of course. She'd drawn on every teaching technique she'd ever learned—plus a few she'd simply made up—since moving in with him, and she knew her efforts had made a difference. Emerson had contributed to the cause, as well. Still, nothing they'd done would have mattered if Royce hadn't decided to come to grips with his blindness.

Royce lopped off the top of his soft-boiled egg with a smooth stroke of his knife. "You've gone back to wearing sneakers," he remarked without preamble. He didn't even turn his head.

"They're athletic shoes," Julia corrected, caught off guard by his opening gambit. She didn't doubt for an instant that rattling her had been Royce's intention. "And I'm back to wearing them because they're comfortable. I'll try to remember to stomp around when I have them on. Or maybe you'd prefer I order a pair of clip-on cleats?"

"I hadn't noticed that my preferences carry much weight with you, Julia." Royce set down the knife. "But given a choice, I'd prefer bells."

"I beg your pardon?"

"Bells," he repeated. An unsettling smile ghosted around the corners of his mouth. "For your shoes." He felt for and found the small spoon resting across the edge of the plate on which the eggcup had been positioned. "Cleats would be hell on the floors and carpets."

Julia shifted in her chair, uncertain how to interpret his tone. She'd spoken the truth about her choice of footwear. Athletic shoes *were* comfortable. They also went with the casual slacks and jeans that made up the bulk of her working wardrobe. Contrary to what Royce apparently assumed, there wasn't anything devious in her decision to wear soft-soled shoes.

At least, not *deliberately* devious.

At that point the door from the kitchen swung open and Emerson walked back into the dining room. "Your breakfast, Miss Kendricks," he announced.

To say the older man took pains with the presentation of her food would be to understate the case. He hovered. He fussed.

"Thank you, Emerson," Julia finally said, trying to convey the message that although she sincerely appreciated his solicitousness, she wanted him to stop what he was doing. Immediately. If not sooner.

"You're welcome," he returned, still fussing. "Might I be asking if you had a pleasant time with Dr. Mitchell last night?"

Julia almost choked at his choice of adjective. *Pleasant?* Lord! Royce had used the same word when he'd asked virtually the same question.

Exactly how much of her foyer encounter with his employer had Emerson witnessed? she wondered uneasily. She'd become aware of the older man's presence when she'd seen the second floor landing light go on. He'd cleared his throat a moment later, then walked down the stairs and calmly asked if he might be of any service. By that time she and Royce had broken their embrace and were standing several feet apart. Even so...

"Yes," Julia managed. "I did."

"They both did," Royce added trenchantly. Steadying the decapitated egg between his left thumb and index finger, he spooned up a bit of its yolk.

"He's an admirable man, Dr. Dennis Mitchell," Emerson commented. "It's no wonder Harvard granted him a full scholarship."

"A full scholarship?" Julia wondered where this exchange was heading.

"Two, actually. One when he was an undergraduate, another when he was admitted to medical school. He didn't mention it to you?"

"Uh, no."

"Typical."

Julia darted a look at Royce. His face was set, his features stony. He was still eating his soft-boiled egg. His movements were controlled, almost mechanical.

She returned her gaze back to the older man. "Emerson—" she began warningly.

"He's never married, you know," Emerson went on reflectively. "Of course, he's not one for socializing. It was a rare thing, his going out to dinner last night. A very rare thing. Not that there aren't dozens of ladies—"

"*Emerson.*"

The older man responded to her imperative tone by glancing from her face to the table and back again. "Oh, I beg your pardon, Miss Kendricks," he said, shifting into the role of attentive servant without missing a beat. "You'll be wanting lemon with your tea, won't you? If you'll excuse me."

And with that, he turned on his heel and left.

Julia almost did. Excuse him, that is. But the moment she heard the door to the kitchen swing shut, she knew she couldn't. Whatever scheme Talley O'Hara Emerson was hatching, she wasn't going to be a party to it.

Crumpling her napkin, Julia dropped it on the table and rose to her feet. "Excuse me, Mr. Williams," she muttered, then stalked off toward the kitchen.

Emerson was closing the door to the refrigerator when Julia walked in on him. He was humming.

"Mr. Emerson," she said.

He turned. His expression was unreadable. "Just Emerson, Miss Kendricks."

Julia's temper ratcheted up a notch or two at this correction. "Fine," she concurred through gritted teeth. "Just Emerson. Tell me, Emerson, just what did you think you were doing in the dining room just now?"

"Why, serving breakfast."

"Besides that."

"Besides that? Really, Miss Kendricks, I'm afraid I don't—"

"Dammit, Emerson!" Julia's self-control snapped. "You were dishing out more than soft-boiled eggs and yogurt a minute ago and you know it!"

There was a long pause. The older man's previously inscrutable expression gave way to something that looked a lot like shock. "You're referring to me wondering about your evening with Dr. Mitchell?"

"That's right."

Julia watched a battle being waged in the depths of Emerson's eyes. Although the contending forces were unclear to her, she sensed the stakes were high. She knew the instant the conflict was settled. But until the older man began to speak again, she had no idea which side had won or why.

"I've known Royce Williams most of his life," Emerson observed slowly. "He's been...well, I've thought of him as a son now and again. If I had to say what drives him, it'd be the need to win."

Julia clenched her hands, her nails digging into her palms. "You're saying your performance in the dining room was intended as some kind of motivational exercise?"

Emerson frowned slightly. "In a sense."

"Royce Williams versus Dennis Mitchell."

The frown deepened. "Well, yes, but—"

"With me as the bone in the dogfight."

Emerson winced. "That's not the way I'd describe—"

"I'm sure it isn't." The words were as bitter as bile. "I'm sure you'd find some nice polite turn of phrase to use. But no matter how you deodorize garbage, Emerson, it still stinks!"

"Miss Kendricks!"

"What do you see when you look at me?" Julia demanded, goaded by emotional demons more than a decade old. They were demons she thought she'd exorcised. Now she knew they'd only been in hiding, waiting to attack. "A blond-haired, blue-eyed bimbo? God knows, you wouldn't be the first. Or maybe I don't even rate that highly with you. Maybe what you see is a cheap little trick. Not a person. Just a good time who can be had by anybody if the price is right. A disposable party favor with n-no real f-feelings—"

She broke off abruptly and turned away. Her throat was tight and dry. Her temples throbbed sickeningly. She could feel her hard-earned self-esteem cracking like plastic veneer.

The truth was obvious and it hurt like hell. Talley O'Hara Emerson had looked at her and he'd seen Juline Fischer.

I can't stay, Julia thought. There's no way I can stay after this, *after last night!*

She'd wanted it. For the first time in her life she'd *wanted* to be kissed and caressed by a man. What's more, she'd wanted to kiss and caress in return. But that wanting had been wrong. And that wrongness had ruined everything.

Voices from the past rose up, clamoring within her brain.

You want it, she heard Wesley Summers grunt. *You want it real bad, sugar, don't you?*

You lying little slut! she heard her mother scream. *Don't you think I know what you want?*

"Miss Kendricks."

Julia shook her head. No, she denied. No. No.

"Miss Kendricks."

Julia shook her head a second time and shrugged off the hand that touched her upper arm. She was trembling.

"Julia."

It wasn't Emerson's unexpected use of her first name that persuaded Julia to turn back to face him. It was his tone of voice. She knew the sound of a person in pain. And as much as she was hurting at that moment, she could tell that Royce Williams's faithful employee was hurting in equal measure.

She didn't speak. She wasn't at all certain she could. She simply looked at the older man and waited.

Emerson cleared his throat. "The afternoon we met," he began, "you asked about my responsibilities here. I told you I do whatever's necessary. Well, I don't always get it right. Knowing what's necessary, that is. And even when I do—" he gestured "— good ends don't justify bad means."

Julia remained silent, her eyes fixed on the older man's face. He sounded sincere. But then again, he'd sounded sincere before.

"You wanted to know what I see when I look at you," Emerson went on, sustaining her gaze. "What I see is a lovely girl who's made something remarkable of her life. A lovely girl who's been able to help a man when no one else could. As for what I was 'dishing out' in the dining room, I'm sorry. From the bottom of my heart, I'm sorry."

Julia finally found her voice. She was torn between fear and a desperate yearning to believe what she'd just heard. "I don't understand," she said. "What made you...I mean, why...?"

"Except for keeping a few medical appointments, Royce hasn't left this house since he was released from the hospital," Emerson replied. "You've seen how it is. He does business on the phone. Anybody but Dr. Mitchell comes to the door, I've got orders to turn them away. And there have been callers. Lots of them. Plus invitations to parties and the like. I was told to dump them in the trash. Before you arrived, I tried everything short of arson to force Royce out. But he wouldn't budge. I'd thought—*hoped*—your having dinner with Dr. Mitchell might encourage him to do the same."

Julia weighed every one of the older man's words. Slowly her mental scale tipped toward trust. Still, she remained wary. "You wanted Royce to accept a date with Dennis?" she asked, seeking refuge in a joke.

For a moment she thought her weak attempt at levity had misfired. Then Emerson's expression eased. "That wasn't my first choice," he answered, a hint of humor rustling through his voice like a breeze through dried leaves. He paused briefly, then went on in an unusually awkward manner. "Just so I'm clear. You and Dr. Mitchell...that is, the two of you aren't, uh..."

"Dennis Mitchell is a good man," Julia said, responding to the question Emerson was having so much trouble articulating. "But the only thing between us is friendship."

Emerson cocked his head. "You must know Royce thinks—"

"He's *blind*," Julia interrupted. The last thing in the world she wanted to do was discuss what she did and didn't know about Royce Williams. "He can't see anything. Especially the truth."

There was an odd, edged silence. Then, "Do you believe *anyone* sees the truth, Miss Kendricks?"

Julia felt herself go pale. "I—I—"

"I'm not certain where I come down on the matter," Emerson continued. "But one thing I see, one thing I believe to be true, is that Royce is very attracted to you."

The blood that had drained out of Julia's face just seconds earlier reversed course and stormed back into her cheeks. "He feels dependent on me," she countered. "And he doesn't like it. He's obviously accustomed to doing for himself. To *being* for himself." She hesitated, then decided she had to go on. "Emerson, what you saw last night in the foyer was, uh, it was—"

"None of my business?"

"Well—"

"What happened in the foyer is between you and Royce, Julia."

"No, it's not!" The contradiction was instinctive. Automatic. It was followed by a gasp of dismay as Julia became aware of the implications of what she'd just said. "Well, yes, it *is* between Roy—Mr. Williams—and me," she quickly admitted. "That is, it *would* be, if there was anything between us. But there isn't."

There was a long pause.

"I see," Emerson eventually replied.

That's all? Julia wondered dizzily. Just "I see"?

The bizarre thing was, she believed the older man did see. Not necessarily what she wanted him to see, of course. But not what she'd feared he saw when she'd castigated him about treating her like a party favor, either.

"I want to help him, Emerson," Julia finally said.

"You already have."

"Not enough."

"More than you know," Emerson disputed. "And in any case, you're not finished yet." He paused, his eyes narrowing. "Are you?"

Just minutes ago Julia had told herself she had no choice but to leave Royce Williams's house. Now she told herself the opposite. She had to stay. She had to do what she'd set out to do.

She also had to make sure that what had happened in the foyer never happened again.

"No," she answered firmly. "I'm not."

"Good." Emerson nodded. "Because I'd be sorry to see you leave. Especially if I thought it was my doing in the dining room that made you decide to go."

"Water under the bridge, Emerson. Forget it."

"A lot of people wouldn't be so forgiving."

"A lot of people haven't had my experience with the road to hell and the good intentions that supposedly pave it."

The corners of the older man's mouth quirked up a millimeter or two, but the expression in his eyes remained serious. "I meant what I said that first time we spoke. Any help you need is yours."

"I know."

"You only have to ask."

"I will, Emerson."

"Thank you." The quirk in his lips relaxed into a genuine curve. "In the meantime, I'll try to stick to serving breakfast and moving the occasional piece of furniture."

Julia had to laugh. "It's a deal."

There was a brief silence. Unlike the ones that had come before, this had a comfortable—even healing—quality about it.

"Well, I'd better get back to the dining room," Julia finally declared. "By the way, don't bother with the lemon."

"The . . . lemon?"

"The lemon for my tea you supposedly came in here to get."

"But you don't—oh." The older man looked abashed.

Julia turned to go. Then an impulse struck her. She pivoted back. "Emerson?"

"Yes, Miss Kendricks?"

"Would you consider calling me Julia again? Maybe? Sometime?"

Talley O'Hara Emerson smiled at her. "I'd consider it an honor."

"I was beginning to think you weren't coming back," Royce said. The dishes he'd been using were pushed away from him. His napkin lay in a wrinkled heap next to his juice glass.

"I'm sorry." Julia slipped back into her chair.

"I was making an observation. Not asking for an apology."

"Oh."

"What were you doing all this time?"

"Talking with Emerson."

"About?" Royce began drumming his fingers on the table.

A tremor of response danced along Julia's nervous system as she watched the rhythmic movement of his fingers. Royce Williams's hands were strong and sinewy. Leanly shaped and lightly dusted with dark hair, they were unmistakably male.

She knew the feel of those masculine hands. It was imprinted on the fragile skin of her face, on the cells of the flesh and blood and bone beneath.

"Julia?"

The sound of Royce's voice was like a pointed stick. Julia was prodded into a degree of candor she'd never intended. "We were talking about your competitive instincts."

Royce stopped drumming on the table. Julia watched him use the fingers of his right hand to feel the face of the watch he had strapped on his left wrist. It was a Braille timepiece, one of the teaching tools she'd brought with her when she'd moved in. Although Royce had mastered it with single-minded swiftness, she couldn't remember having seen him "read" it without her prompting.

"You talked about my competitive instincts for *fifteen* minutes?"

"Among other things."

"I don't like being discussed behind my back."

Something strange stirred deep within Julia. It felt a bit like the impulse to tease she occasionally felt toward her self-proclaimed brothers, Peter, Ty and Lee. "Rest assured, you weren't the only topic on the agenda," she said.

"Oh, really?" Royce's voice roughened. "Who else was on it?"

For the first time in her life, Julia Kendricks sensed the power a woman could wield over a man. It was scary. But it was seductive, too. Without really considering the consequences, she surrendered to lure and replied, "Dennis Mitchell."

The fingers of Royce's right hand clenched with convulsive force. A flash of alarm streaked through Julia. She lowered her gaze.

There was a long silence. Then, "About last night..."

Julia's head came up with a jerk. "That's forgotten."

"Not by me it isn't."

Her heart lurched as Royce turned in his chair. His eyes fixed on her face. The intensity of his stare was such that for one wild instant she was utterly convinced he must have re-gained his sight.

Julia ran her tongue over her lips. Her cheeks were burn-ing. "Nothing happened," she asserted with all the convic-tion she could muster.

Royce remained silent. He just kept looking.

"Mr. Williams—"

"Last night you called me Royce," he said softly.

"I—I did?"

"Oh, yes. You most certainly did."

Memory came flooding back. She *had* called him Royce. Her voice had been breathless and her palms had been pressed flat against his broad chest when she'd done it. She'd told herself she was trying to push him away. But in her heart of hearts she'd known this was a lie.

"I liked the way it sounded, Julia," Royce added. "I'd like to hear you do it again."

Julia knew there were a million reasons why she couldn't do as he was suggesting. Unfortunately she couldn't seem to summon a single one of those reasons to mind.

"Please?"

The breath Julia hadn't known she was holding escaped in a whoosh. "Now, why," she said shakily, "do I have the feeling that's a word you don't use very often?"

It was a stupid thing to ask and she realized it the mo-ment the words left her lips. Aghast, she opened her mouth to try to take them back. Royce forestalled her.

"Probably because you've been around me long enough to discover that I can be an unmitigated bastard, even un-der the best of circumstances," he replied. Where his tone had been soft, it was now pure steel.

Julia blinked, bewildered by his mercurial shift of mood. "W-what?"

"I was quoting Dennis."

"Dennis Mitchell called you an unmitigated bastard?"

Royce shrugged. "He told me I could be. Implying, I suppose, that there are moments when I'm not."

"When was this?"

"Yesterday. Shortly before he asked me what I'd say to the idea of his inviting you to dinner."

"You're telling me *he* asked *you*—"

"Julia." Royce leaned forward. Once again, he seemed to look directly at her. "Dennis was right about me. And Emerson was right about him. He's a good man. One of the best."

Julia had the oddest feeling she'd just received an apology. A very oblique apology, to be sure, but an apology nonetheless.

"Is that why you practically forced me to go out with him?" she asked after a few seconds. "Because you're an unmitigated bastard, and he's a Boy Scout?"

Royce said nothing.

"I didn't want to go," she emphasized.

"Didn't you?"

"No. I didn't."

"But you *did* have a pleasant time with him."

Julia gestured, exasperated beyond the limits of discretion. "Did it ever occur to you that I might have had a pleasant time with *you* if you'd been the one I'd had dinner with?"

"Pleasant isn't the word that comes immediately to mind, no." The response was somewhere between insulting and suggestive.

She gasped.

"I'm sorry," Royce said quickly.

Sorry wasn't good enough. "For what?"

Royce closed his eyes, a hint of vulnerability shadowing his strong features. "Anything you want," he answered. "Anything at all."

Julia's anger drained away. She reached out for Royce in the same impulsive fashion she had done days ago in the upstairs hallway. But this time good sense overrode instinct at the very last second. She pulled her hand back, shaken by the realization of what she'd almost done.

Taking a deep breath, she searched for some kind of balance. "What I want," she said carefully, "is to help you."

Royce opened his eyes. They were very dark. "Why?"

Julia trembled on the brink of telling him the truth for one dizzying instant, then retreated.

"Julia?"

She cleared her throat. "Because you need it."

The vulnerability disappeared from Royce's features. "Fair enough," he replied after several moments.

There was yet another long silence. Julia used it to try to figure out exactly what the phrase "fair enough" was supposed to signify. Her mind kept returning to the comment Dennis had made about Royce Williams not always meaning what he said . . . or saying what he meant.

"Julia?"

She stiffened. "What?"

"Are you going for a walk today?"

"Are you trying to get rid of me?"

"Actually, I was hoping you might invite me to join you."

Julia's pulse accelerated with a wild hop, skip, and jump. Her breathing pattern altered sharply. "And if I did?"

Royce's smile sent a quicksilver thrill coursing through her veins. "There's only one way to find out, isn't there?"

Seven

"**W**here are we?"

Royce cocked his head, listening to the passing cars. He was definitely getting better at sorting out traffic noises and using them to orient himself, he decided. As long as there wasn't a lot of wind. Wind distorted the sounds he was learning to rely on. He'd discovered this unpleasant fact of sightless life while he and Julia were out walking the day before. Today, thank heaven, the weather was barely breezy.

"Royce? Do you know where we are?"

Although Julia had been addressing him by his first name for a week, Royce still took pleasure in hearing her do so. There were times when he wondered whether this pleasure wasn't a little too intense.

"Lost," he answered dryly.

Julia gave a throaty laugh. "This *is* your neighborhood."

"Yes, well, I never really paid much attention to it when I could see." He felt a curious pang of regret as he spoke.

"Map it out in your head," Julia urged.

Royce tapped his cane against the sidewalk, mentally retracing the route they'd taken when they'd left the town house. "The corner of Boylston and Arlington," he said confidently. "The Unitarian Universalist Church should be over there—" he gestured "—and the Public Garden is across the street."

"Exactly."

They began walking again. Royce swung his cane from side to side, testing the path ahead. His left arm was bent, his hand clasping Julia's arm just above the elbow. They were barely half a step apart.

"Do you ever feel awkward doing this?" he asked, conscious of how smoothly their movements seemed to mesh. He'd experienced an unnerving sense of connection the first time he'd taken hold of Julia outside the town house. Given the passionate kiss they'd shared in the foyer, the contact should have seemed impersonal. But it hadn't. Touching her—*trusting* her—had stirred him in a way he couldn't explain. And he'd sensed it had stirred her, too.

"Doing what?"

"Leading a blind man around."

"It's not leading. It's guiding."

"Same thing."

"Not at all."

They walked in silence for a minute or so. Then Julia announced that there was a curb ahead. Royce managed the shift of terrain smoothly.

"The last week I was in the hospital I got sick of using bedpans," he remarked. "I asked an orderly to help me to the bathroom. He took my arm, then tried to steer me in the right direction by pushing. I felt like a grocery cart."

"A lot of sighted people do that the first time they try to help someone who's visually handicapped."

"Did you?"

Julia laughed. The sound teased along Royce's nerve endings. "The first blind person I tried to help was Peter. He wasn't at all shy about telling me what I was supposed to do and how I was supposed to do it."

Royce's brain automatically slotted the name into place. He knew Peter was Julia's fifteen-year-old brother. The boy who'd been born into a world of perpetual darkness.

Peter was the first member of Julia's family she'd mentioned to him. It had happened the second time they'd gone out walking. The reference had been full of affection. It had been obvious to Royce that while young Peter lacked the ability to see, he did not lack the ability to inspire love.

Bits and pieces of Julia's background had come out during subsequent outings. It seemed the farther they walked together, the more intimate their conversations became.

Royce had learned that Julia's father had died when she was ten and that she still felt the loss. He wasn't certain what had become of her mother. However, he had deduced that even if the woman were alive, her estrangement from Julia was total.

He knew Julia had two brothers, Ty and Lee, in addition to Peter. She'd said they were both eighteen, so he assumed they must be twins. She'd also spoken about a set of foster parents, John and Emily. Her devotion to them had been clear in every word she'd uttered.

Oddly, her comments about John and Emily had started Royce thinking about his long relationship with Emerson. And once he'd started thinking about it, he'd found himself driven to talk about it, as well. That, inevitably, had led to his revealing a few truths about his family life—or lack of it.

All this wasn't to imply that the two of them had poured out their hearts during their walks around Boston's Back Bay. They hadn't. Julia was as adept at changing subjects as anyone Royce had ever met. And he—well, he'd spent a lifetime learning how to protect his innermost feelings. Still, there was no denying that they'd begun to open up to each other.

Nor was there any denying that Royce's response to this mutual lowering of defenses was decidedly mixed. While he wanted to know more about Julia and to have her know more about him, he was deeply wary of taking on the emotional responsibility that went with sharing secrets.

"Have you given any more thought to getting a dog, Royce?" Julia asked suddenly.

Royce forced himself to refocus on exactly where he was and what he was doing. He'd let his attention drift, relying on Julia to see that he didn't stumble into trouble. He had to stop doing that, he warned himself. Accepting her help was one thing. Becoming dependent on her was entirely another.

"Yes," he replied tersely.

"Yes, what?"

"Yes, I've thought about it some more."

"And?"

"No. No dog." His mind was made up. He'd taken Julia's arm and let her "guide" him because he knew he'd be able to let go of her—permanently—when his vision returned. Same with using the cane. The moment his sight came back, it would be tossed in the trash. But when it came to agreeing to a Seeing Eye dog...

"Have you ever had a dog?"

"Once. His name was Beacon. He ran off when I went away to school."

"I'm sorry."

"Why?" He grimaced. "You weren't responsible."

"Neither were you."

Royce felt his throat close up. It had been years since he'd thought about Beacon. Or, rather, years since he'd permitted himself to do so. "I left him, didn't I?"

"You were just a little boy!"

Royce stopped dead in his tracks. He felt Julia halt, too. Then he sensed her shifting around to face him. "What makes you say that?" he asked.

There was a long pause. Royce envisioned Julia's blue-green eyes darting back and forth as she debated how to answer his question. He pictured her nibbling on her lower lip or fiddling with a strand of her pale hair.

"Julia?" he prompted.

He heard her sigh. "The night I had dinner with Dennis Mitchell, he mentioned that your father sent you to some military academy when you were only eight years old. I just assumed—"

"I seem to remember telling you I don't like being discussed behind my back."

"For heaven's sake, Royce! The one thing Dennis and I really have in common is you. It's perfectly natural that your name would come up during a conversation."

"There's a considerable difference between mentioning my name in passing and reviewing my school records, Julia."

"Dennis didn't reveal your grade-point average if that's what you're worried about."

Royce didn't give a damn about his GPA. What he did care about was the defensiveness he heard in Julia's voice. He'd pretty much accepted that his initial reading of the relationship between her and Dennis had been wrong. There was nothing sexual there. But there was *something* between them. More than an understanding, yet not quite a conspiracy. It was a kind of complicity. And deep in his gut he knew it had to do with him.

"Dennis and I have you in common," he pointed out trenchantly. "How would you feel if you discovered *we'd* been talking about *you?*"

"What do you mean 'if'?" Julia parried. "You admitted Dennis asked your permission before he invited me out to dinner last week. If *that* doesn't constitute *talking* about me—"

Royce had to laugh. He didn't want to, but the deft way she'd turned the verbal tables on him made it impossible not to. "Touché," he said.

After a moment or two they began walking again. They were on Newbury Street now, Royce calculated, although he wasn't completely sure.

"I *am* sorry about Beacon," Julia told him.

"It was a long time ago," he replied with a shrug, closing his mind to the all-too-vivid image of the beribboned mongrel pup that had reduced him to a state of speechless joy on the morning of his seventh birthday. He also tried, less successfully, to shut out the echoes of the argument he'd eavesdropped on many hours later.

"But, Archer," he'd heard his mother say. "Royce wanted a puppy so much. It was the only thing he asked for."

"Since when are children supposed to get everything they want?" his father had challenged coldly. "*I* certainly didn't. I thought I'd made my feelings on this dog issue quite clear, Margaret."

"You did, I—I suppose," had come the faltering reply. "But, darling, did you see Royce's face? Did you see how *thrilled* he was?"

"Thrilled about a mangy mutt from the pound? That *is* where you got that animal, isn't it?"

"I'm not certain. Emerson picked—"

"A *servant* gave my son a dog I didn't want him to have?"

"*No!*" His mother had sounded genuinely alarmed. Royce remembered having been afraid, too, but not understanding why. "No, Archer. I *asked* Emerson to find a puppy for Royce. He only did—"

"*Royce!*"

This sudden cry, and a sharp yank on his arm, hauled Royce out of the past and back into the present. He checked his step in the same instant his ears told him what he'd been on the verge of doing.

"You almost stepped in front of a car!" Julia exclaimed. Her voice was shaking.

"So I just heard," Royce replied, feeling slightly sick.

"You *have* to concentrate, Royce!"

"I know." He silently cursed the darkness he was trapped in. "I'm sorry."

"I don't want you to apologize. I want you to pay attention!"

The intensity of Julia's tone sent a tremor of reaction skittering up Royce's spine. She cares, he realized with a shock. She genuinely cares what happens to me.

But *why?* he had to ask himself, returning to the question that had plagued him almost since her arrival. The concern he felt from Julia went beyond a passionate devotion to her work. It was personal.

Yet "personal" made no sense. What had he ever done for Julia Kendricks that she should give a damn whether he lived or died? Heaven knew, he'd behaved like the unmitigated bastard Dennis had accused him of being during much of the time she'd been living under his roof. He'd taken out his frustrations on her more times than he could count. He'd even let his libido off the leash—

"Royce?" The temper was gone from Julia's voice.

He took a steadying breath. "What?"

"I'm sorry," she said. "I shouldn't have yelled at you."

Royce's memory cartwheeled back. He heard his mother pleading with his father. Trying to placate him. Practically abasing herself in an effort to defuse his anger.

Dear God, he thought, appalled. *Does Julia honestly believe that's what I want from her? Does she think I'm like...* him?

Royce lifted his left hand. He sought Julia's face, brushing his gloved fingertips gently against her cheek.

"I'm the one who was in the wrong, Julia," he said. "And I'd hardly call what you did yelling."

"But—" Her voice was several notes lower than normal.

"Shh." He shifted his hand slightly, sealing her mouth. "Aren't blind people supposed to have much sharper hearing than sighted people? I may be in the dark about a lot of things at this point, but I can definitely tell the difference between yelling and not yelling."

After a moment he felt her lips relax into the beginning of a smile. He took his hand away, lowering it so he could take her arm once again.

"That's not necessarily true, you realize," Julia eventually observed. There was still an extra hint of huskiness in her voice.

"What?"

"That people who're visually impaired have a higher degree of auditory acuity than those who aren't."

"You mean, I'm not going to develop sonar?" The realization that he was joking about the implications of his disability startled him. But it felt right to do so.

"Not unless you plan to turn into a bat."

He feigned a grimace of disappointment. "What about being able to identify smells with a single sniff?"

"I think that would depend on the smell."

The admission that he would be able to identify her scent anywhere, anytime, trembled on the tip of Royce's tongue.

He forced himself to swallow it, not wanting to jeopardize the return to amity he'd engineered.

"Guide on, Miss Kendricks," he requested after a few moments, gripping her arm.

She did.

The closer they got to the town house, the more familiar the terrain felt to Royce. Sensations coming from the tip of his cane and through the soles of his shoes told him he was on home turf.

The sound of frantic barking from somewhere off to his right reminded him of something they'd discussed earlier. It also renewed a sense of curiosity he'd felt from the first moment Julia had mentioned her youngest brother.

"Does your brother have a Seeing Eye dog?" he asked.

"Uh-huh. A German shepherd. His name is Amadeus."

"Peter likes Mozart, I take it?"

"And rock and rap and reggae. And every type of music in between." Julia sounded proud. "Peter's a very talented musician. He was selected for a special program at Julliard last summer. The school's asked him back for this summer, but he hasn't made up his mind yet." She paused briefly. Royce sensed she was smiling. "He claims he's considering his options. I think he's hoping one of those heavy metal groups will need a new keyboard player."

They continued walking.

"My mother was musical," Royce said.

"Was she?" The response was encouraging without being overly inquisitive.

"Mmm. She had aspirations to be a concert pianist."

"She must have been very good."

"I never really heard her play." The admission did not come easily. "My father didn't approve of it."

"Why not?"

"I'm not sure. Maybe he was jealous of how much it meant to her. Or of the attention it brought her. My father had a problem with what he called 'showing off.' He thought it was vulgar." Royce grimaced. "Not worthy of a Williams, if you know what I mean."

"So your mother gave up playing the piano?"

"I don't think she had much choice."

"It must have been hard for her."

"She got involved with the Boston Symphony and the Handel and Haydn Society. Running fund-raisers. Coordinating educational programs. That sort of thing."

"Activities worthy of a Williams?"

"Oh, yes," he agreed sardonically. Then he sighed. "She was very good at what she did. Even my father said so. But now I can't help wondering how much it must have hurt her to be relegated to applauding *other* people's music."

"Are you musical?" Julia asked.

"Lord, no. Although I am on the symphony board."

"Because of your mother?"

Royce nodded slowly. "It meant a lot to her. And when it comes to the board, my inability to carry a tune in a bucket is more than offset by my willingness to write big checks." He fell silent for a few steps, then asked, "What about you?"

"Oh, I'd definitely be willing to write big checks for good causes if I thought my bank would honor them," Julia quipped.

Royce smiled. "I meant, what about you and music? Does musical talent run in the Kendricks family?"

She seemed to tense for an instant. Then she gave a little laugh and replied, "I'm very good at listening."

"So I've noticed."

"I learned a lot about it from Peter."

Royce spent a moment debating whether to ask the question he'd been puzzling over for nearly a week. He finally decided to take the risk. "Does Peter realize he's different from most people?"

"You mean, does he know most people can see?"

Julia's bluntness surprised him for a second, then he realized it was very much in character. "Yes," he said.

"Peter knows," his companion answered serenely. "But he doesn't really understand. He can't imagine what seeing is."

"You're saying he doesn't miss what he's never experienced."

"I'm saying he experiences the world in his own way, Royce. Even without being able to see, Peter is one of the most observant people I've ever known. He doesn't take *anything* for granted.''

"He's lucky," Royce said. There was a knot in his chest. His throat was tight.

"What do you mean?"

"I've learned a lot about myself since the accident, Julia," he confessed quietly. "Damned little of it pleasant. But the hardest thing I've had to face is that I spent thirty-six years looking at the world without really seeing it. I was blind to my life long before I lost my sight."

"Is this all right, Emerson?" Julia asked two nights later. She fiddled with the draped skirt of the long-sleeved, wool crepe dress she'd purchased just a few hours ago, wondering for the thousandth time if she was making a terrible mistake.

The older man surveyed her from head to toe. "Plain," he declared in a judicious tone. "But perfect."

"Let me guess," Royce said from a few feet behind Julia. "It's basic black."

Julia pivoted abruptly, her right hand going to her breast. She'd been so wrapped up in her anxiety about her appearance that she hadn't heard Royce coming down the stairs.

Her breath seemed to wedge at the top of her throat. He looked...Lord! The only words she could think of were "tall, dark and handsome." She'd seen photographs of Royce Archer Williams dressed for a night on the town over the years, of course. But as striking as some of those society page pictures had been, they paled in comparison with in-the-flesh reality.

The tuxedo Royce was wearing was obviously custom-tailored. The elegant severity of the garment underscored the innate power of his leanly muscled body. A pair of dark glasses lent a dangerous edge of glamour to the compelling aura of masculinity that surrounded him.

"Well?" he asked. "Am I right? Basic black?"

"Positively nunlike," Emerson confirmed.

"I told you this morning I don't go for glitz," Julia said, lowering her hand and raising her chin.

"No need for you to," Emerson responded. "Spangles and the like are for women who want their *dresses* to be noticed, not them."

"I hadn't realized fashion philosophy was one of your specialties, Emerson," Royce remarked.

"I've learned a thing or two in my time."

"Including the combination to the safe in the study?"

Emerson frowned. Julia thought he looked as mystified by this query as she was. Then, suddenly, his face relaxed into a knowing smile. "I think I could call it to mind."

Julia's gaze bounced back to Royce. He, too, was smiling. "Good," he said. "There's a medium-size jeweler's case—"

"I know what you're wanting. I'll be right back."

"Royce," Julia began uneasily as the older man made his exit. "I don't think—"

"Of course you do."

"I—" She broke off. "What's that supposed to mean?"

"Think about it, Miss Kendricks."

Julia stared at him, conscious of a fluttering in her stomach. Royce was in a peculiar mood. In fact, now that she considered it, he'd been in a peculiar mood ever since she'd agreed to go to the symphony with him this evening.

Well, actually, "agreed to go" was less than accurate. She'd been manipulated into accepting his invitation and she knew it.

She and Royce had been finishing breakfast when Emerson had taken it upon himself to mention that there was a special concert at Symphony Hall that evening. He'd also taken it upon himself to offer the opinion that, as a member of the symphony board, Royce really ought to go.

One thing had led inevitably to another. Royce had concurred with Emerson's assessment of his social obligations with one proviso: Julia had to attend the concert, as well.

That had precipitated a discussion—an argument, really—about her wardrobe.

"Now where have I heard that before?" Royce had drawled after she'd protested that she had nothing appropriate to wear.

Julia had flushed, knowing he was referring to the desperate excuse she'd offered to avoid going to dinner with Dennis Mitchell. But she'd persevered. "I came here prepared to work, Royce," she'd countered. "Not to attend gala events at Symphony Hall."

"So go out and buy something. I've got accounts at all the—"

"No!"

Her refusal of his offer had been as intemperate as it was instinctive. She'd seen Royce stiffen. She'd watched his brows vee together as his forehead furrowed. She'd sensed him factoring her response in with all the other impressions he'd gathered about her.

"No, what?" Royce had asked after a few moments.

"No, I am not going to let you buy me a dress."

"Not even if I want to?"

Her heart had skipped a beat. "Nobody pays for—"

The sound of her name pulled her back into the present.

"What?" she asked, her gaze flying to Royce's face.

"I wanted to know whether I pass inspection." If Royce had noticed her detour down memory lane, he gave no sign of it. "For all the confidence I have in the way you and Emerson reorganized my closet, I still feel a little anxious about missing buttons and mismatched clothes. I'd hate to go to Symphony Hall with my fly open or wearing chartreuse socks."

Julia moistened her lips and patted at her hair. She'd pinned it up for the evening, much as she'd done the night she'd had dinner with Dennis Mitchell. "You look fine," she said after a moment. "Very polished."

"And the shades?" He indicated the sunglasses.

"Um—"

At that point, Emerson returned. He crossed to Royce and handed him a palm-size rectangular box covered with black velvet. He stepped back. Royce fumbled with the snap-hinged case for a moment, then opened it. He extended it toward Julia.

For all that she was braced to resist and reject, Julia gasped when she saw what he was offering. She couldn't help it.

Nestled inside the box on a cushion of creamy white satin were two perfectly matched black baroque pearls dangling from two delicately curved clusters of platinum-set diamonds. They were the most exquisite pair of earrings Julia had ever seen.

"These were my mother's," Royce told her quietly. "I'd like you to wear them tonight."

Julia glanced at Emerson. He was staring at the earrings, his craggy face revealing a startling mixture of longing and loss. Then he seemed to sense her scrutiny. He shifted his gaze from the box in Royce's hand to her face, his expression coalescing into an impenetrable mask.

"I—I can't," Julia said after a moment, looking back at Royce. Dear God, she thought, was it possible that Talley O'Hara Emerson and Margaret Williams had been—

"If your ears have lobes, you most certainly can," Royce returned.

Julia shook her head. "That's not what I mean, Royce," she said, struggling to keep her voice steady. "These earrings—"

"These earrings have been locked away since my mother died. I think she'd approve of their getting out and about again."

She was wavering and she knew it. The lure of the earrings' beauty was almost irresistible. "What if I lose them?"

"They're insured."

"But—"

"*Please,* Julia."

She caught her breath, then acquiesced. "All...all right."

With trembling fingers, she took the earrings out of their satin cocoon and fastened them into place.

Royce turned, handing the empty jeweler's case back to Emerson. As he did so, Julia caught a glimpse of herself in the lenses of his glasses. She had the disorienting impression the reflection she saw was that of a stranger.

She looked questioningly at Emerson. "The earrings. Are they—?"

"They suit you very well, Julia," was all he said.

Eight

The concert was wonderful.

Julia was familiar with the Boston Symphony Orchestra, of course. Its work was well represented in Peter's massive collection of records, tapes and CDs. But there was something special about hearing a live performance, especially at Symphony Hall.

The evening's guest soloist was a doll-like Japanese-American violinist. When she initially walked out on stage, Julia was certain she must be younger than the sixteen years the program proclaimed her to be. Then the girl began to play. Within a matter of measures, Julia knew she was hearing a talent that transcended age.

It was almost a shock when the house lights came up for intermission. Julia felt an aching emptiness. She yearned for the break to be over so the music could begin again.

Compelled by an urge to share what she was feeling, Julia turned toward Royce. He was seated on her right. His dark head was bent, his shoulders rigidly set. His arms were braced, his hands cupped his knees.

"Royce?" she asked anxiously. "Are you all right?"

His head snapped up. "Sorry," he apologized with a crooked smile. "But it's tough to go from that—" he nodded toward the stage "—to this." He gestured vaguely at their fellow symphony-goers.

Startled at hearing her own emotions put into words, Julia found herself returning Royce's smile. It was a pointless thing to do, given his blindness. Yet her mouth seemed to curve upward of its own accord.

"I know," she concurred feelingly. "One minute you're in musical paradise, the next minute you're—"

"Excuse us. We'd like to get by."

The impatient request came from a bulky older woman in midnight blue brocade. She was accompanied by an equally corpulent man in a tuxedo.

"Oh, of course," Julia said quickly. As she stood to allow the couple to pass, she glanced back to her right. "Royce—"

He was already on his feet, feeling his way toward the aisle. After a fractional hesitation, Julia followed him.

"Royce?" the woman in brocade demanded in a loud voice as she squeezed her way out of the row of chairs. "Royce Williams?"

Julia saw what looked like a flash of distaste streak across Royce's face. A split second later, his angular features were disciplined into unreadability. "That's right, Mrs. Hitchens," he affirmed.

"Hilly, look," the woman said to her portly escort. "It's Royce Williams!"

The two men exchanged polite greetings and rather awkward handshakes. Then Royce introduced Julia. The Hitchens—Cecelia and Hilliard—acknowledged her presence, but that was about all.

"This is so unexpected," Cecelia confided, enunciating each word with great care. "Running into you this evening, I mean. Why, Hilly and I didn't even *see* you—" The older woman broke off abruptly, her plump cheeks turning scarlet. "Oh," she gasped. "Oh, Lord! I'm *terribly* sorry. I didn't intend—"

"No need to apologize," Royce replied with sardonic courtesy. "I didn't see you, either."

The older woman started as though she'd been smacked in the face with a dead fish. Then she gave a forced-sounding laugh. Hilly joined in with a tight little chuckle. Julia saw the two exchange uneasy glances.

"Very amusing," Cecelia said in a tone that suggested just the opposite. She leaned in toward Royce and raised her voice again. "I was so upset to hear about your accident, Royce. How *are* you?"

"Well, I'm not deaf," Royce returned. His teeth flashed, white and slightly wicked. "At least, not yet."

The older woman pulled back, her expression bewildered. "Of course you're not deaf!" she declared. "I never thought—"

"Cecelia dear, I think we'd better be going," Hilly interrupted firmly. "Libby and Albert will be waiting for us in the lobby. And I'm certain Royce and Miss, uh, Miss Kendricks would like to get some refreshments before the intermission's over."

"Oh." Cecelia made a fluttery gesture with her right hand. "Oh, yes, of course." Another flutter. "Well, goodbye, Royce."

"Goodbye," Royce answered.

Hilliard Hitchens latched onto his wife's pudgy arm and began to lead her away. "Hope to see you again!" Cecelia trilled over her shoulder, waggling her sausagelike fingers.

"Not if I see you first," Julia muttered. Then she blinked, realizing Royce had murmured the same words at the same time. "Royce—"

"Great minds think alike," he remarked wryly, seeking and finding her arm. She could feel the warmth of his hand through the fine fabric of her tight-fitting sleeve. A tremor of response skittered through her as he stroked the crook of her elbow with his fingertips. "Would you like a drink?"

An emotion Julia couldn't put a name to stirred deep within her. It seemed to expand, balloonlike, until it filled her chest. "Actually," she said a bit breathlessly, "I think I'd like two or three."

They had several more encounters with people Royce knew before they managed to reach the lobby and secure some refreshments for themselves. On the whole, Julia thought Royce handled himself with considerably more aplomb than most of his acquaintances.

"I seem to be making people uncomfortable," he observed, taking a healthy swallow from the glass of champagne he was holding in his left hand. "Is it the cane, the sunglasses, or a problem with personal hygiene?"

"I have the feeling making people uncomfortable isn't an entirely new experience for you," Julia sidestepped, matching his tone. The past few minutes had shown her an aspect of Royce's character she'd never really seen. While she'd long since gauged the strength of his personality, she'd never realized he was capable of dominating—even dwarfing—other men with a few words. The odd thing was, she wasn't certain he knew how intimidating he could be.

Unbidden, her mind flashed back more than ten years. She remembered Royce's low, authoritative voice telling her that things were all right. She also remembered thinking that he sounded as though he was accustomed to having what he said believed simply because he was the one who said it.

"Point well taken," Royce replied, his mouth twisting with a trace of self-mockery. "Let me rephrase. I have the distinct impression I'm making people even *more* uncomfortable than usual this evening."

"A lot of people who don't have physical disabilities have problems dealing with people who do," Julia tried to explain. "They feel uneasy. Self-conscious. They're worried about doing something that will make them seem insensitive."

Royce shook his head. "There's more to it than that, Julia. The vibes I'm getting are . . . are . . ." He shook his head a second time, obviously frustrated by his inability to express what he was sensing from other people.

Julia sighed, knowing they were marching into a psychological bramble patch. Several courses in her special education training had involved examining the very contradictory responses contemporary society had toward the blind—indeed, toward all individuals with disabilities. These classes had prompted her to take a long, hard look at her own attitudes about physical and mental handicaps.

"Part of what you're picking up is something I call the there-but-for-the-grace-of-God-go-I response," she told Royce. "Or, to put it less charitably, the better-you-than-me syndrome. It's a very human reaction. But people tend to feel guilty if they realize they're experiencing it and *that* tends to make them feel angry and awkward. At the same time, there seems to be this *anxiety* that one person's misfortune might rub off on somebody else."

"In other words, people are afraid that handicaps might be contagious."

Julia sighed. "More or less, yes."

Royce took another drink of his champagne. "My father was a great believer in Darwinian theory," he commented reflectively. "Survival of the fittest and all that. He wasn't very tolerant of weakness."

"I'd gotten the impression your father wasn't very tolerant of anything," Julia replied. Then she bit her lip, wondering whether she'd gone too far. Her anxiety eased when Royce gave a rueful laugh.

"True," he agreed. "I wonder what he'd make of tonight's soloist."

"That she's a genius?" Julia was thankful for the opportunity to shift to another topic of conversation.

Royce's mouth relaxed into a smile. "She *is* remarkable, isn't she? When she performed that concerto..." He paused, seeming to savor the memory. "I felt as though I was hearing the piece for the first time."

"I can't believe she's only sixteen."

"Age has nothing to do with a talent like hers."

Julia's heart missed a beat. For the second time in just a few minutes, Royce had articulated *her* thoughts, *her* feelings! She opened her mouth to tell him as much but was forestalled by the sudden materialization of a stunningly beautiful redhead.

"Royce!" the woman exclaimed, going up on tiptoe to kiss him. She left a small smear of lipstick on his cheek, like a brand. "Darling!"

Although they'd never met, the redhead was not a stranger to Julia. She'd seen her in a number of the society page photographs of Royce she'd collected. Her name was

Stephanie Talcott. The only child of socially prominent parents, she had married extremely well and divorced even better.

"Hello, Stephanie," Royce responded, rubbing the place she'd kissed with his fingertips. He seemed indulgently accepting of the impetuous greeting he'd just received. Julia had the feeling Ms. Talcott elicited that kind of response from most members of the opposite sex.

"I tried to phone you from Europe while you were in the hospital, you know," Stephanie declared. "But the switchboard would never put me through. Then when I got back from London last week, I stopped by your town house to wish you a happy New Year. Emerson told me you couldn't be disturbed."

Her dazzling green-gold eyes flicked toward Julia at this point. Julia sustained the woman's scrutiny with what she hoped was a polite expression. She had to struggle to keep from smiling when she realized that the redhead had homed in on Margaret Williams's diamond and pearl earrings. While Stephanie Talcott might not know their pedigree, the sudden arching of her brows made it plain that she had a very accurate idea of their price.

"I appreciate the thought," Royce said. "But I haven't been seeing people since I came home."

Stephanie's gaze flew back to his face. "How can you *joke* about what's happened?" she demanded. Then she frowned. She took a step back. "The sunglasses. Oh, Royce. You weren't...scarred...in the accident, were you?"

"Not so you'd notice," he answered. A moment later Julia felt his left hand reclaim the crook of her right elbow. "I'd like to introduce you to someone who's been working with me during the past few weeks. This is Julia Kendricks. Julia, Stephanie Talcott."

"How do you do, Ms. Talcott," Julia said after a moment.

"Ms. Kendricks," Stephanie responded. Her gaze dropped, clearly noting the physical contact between Royce and Julia, then bounced back up. "You're...what?" she inquired. "The human equivalent of a Seeing Eye dog?"

"Oh, hardly a *dog,* darling."

This drawled reproof came from a languidly handsome man who'd just strolled up behind Stephanie. He flashed a wafer-thin smile at Julia.

"Cutter," Stephanie said, turning her classically coiffed head and showing her perfectly polished teeth. "I was wondering where you were."

"Were you really, Steffie?" the man countered. "Well, all you had to do was to look over your shoulder as you dashed off in hot pursuit of Royce and you would have seen me standing exactly where you abandoned me."

"Still practicing the fine art of losing friends and alienating people, Cutter?" Royce interpolated. He sounded amused. Slanting a glance at him, Julia was surprised to see that he *looked* amused, as well.

"Oh, absolutely," Cutter replied. "And if I practice enough, I may get it right one of these days." He paused for a moment. When he went on, his voice was free of its previous acidity. "I'm sorry about your accident, Royce. And I'm sorry about not getting in touch. But frankly, I didn't know what to say."

"How unusual," Stephanie sniped.

"Indeed, darling," Cutter concurred blandly. He shifted his attention back to Julia. "Cutter Dane," he said, extending a well-manicured hand. "I'm Steffie's escort of last resort. Her mother was my second stepfather's first wife. Or was it her stepmother who was my father's second wife? In any case, I'm extremely presentable. As unlikely as it may seem, I prepped with Royce."

Julia shook the proffered hand. "I'm Julia Kendricks, Mr. Dane."

"Yes, so I heard before I interrupted." He gave her another wafer-thin smile. "Tell me, Miss—it *is* Miss, I gather?—Kendricks. Exactly what is it you do with...or for...Royce?"

"Think of it as the blonde guiding the blind, Cutter," Royce answered before Julia had a chance to respond.

"You know what she looks like?" Stephanie questioned suspiciously.

Julia felt Royce's fingers tighten against her arm. She looked up at him. His head was turned toward her. Once again, she saw her reflection in the lenses of his dark glasses. Once again, she had the disorienting impression that she was gazing at the face of a woman she barely knew.

Royce smiled at her. Straight at her. The slow curving of his lips sent a wave of heat rushing up into her cheeks.

"Royce?" the redhead prodded.

"Let's just say my vision of Julia Kendricks is getting clearer all the time," he replied.

It was dangerous to ask, and Julia realized it. But not asking—*not knowing*—seemed even riskier.

"Royce?"

"Yes?"

They were standing in the foyer of his town house, less than two feet apart. Julia had finished securing the locks on the front door just moments before. The instant she'd heard the thunk of the dead bolt sliding into place, she'd made up her mind what she had to do.

"What did you mean?"

There. It was finally out. The question she'd been puzzling over ever since Royce had made his extraordinary comment about his "vision" of her.

Royce cocked his head. Although he'd removed his coat, he hadn't taken off his sunglasses. Julia fervently wished he would.

"What do you mean, what did I mean?" he countered.

"What you said to Stephanie Talcott earlier this evening." She glanced away. "About your vision of me getting clearer all the time."

"Ah, that."

"Yes, that." Julia forced herself to look at Royce once again. She tried to fix her gaze on his nose but it kept drifting downward to his mouth. She moistened her lips with a quick flick of her tongue, conscious of a sudden acceleration in her heartbeat. "What did you mean by it?"

No answer. No change in his expression, either.

"Royce?"

"What did you think of Stephanie?" he asked.

Julia stiffened, genuinely taken aback. "I thought she was stunning," she replied after a few seconds. She'd thought a few other things as well, of course, but she wasn't about to admit it.

Royce nodded. Julia wasn't certain whether he was endorsing her assessment or simply acknowledging the fact that she'd offered it.

"Stephanie's accustomed to being the center of attention," he observed after a brief silence. "She's also used to being the most attractive woman in any given crowd."

"So?"

"So—" one corner of Royce's mouth kicked up "—she gets unpleasant when there's competition."

It took Julia a moment to grasp what he was saying.

Stephanie Talcott had been unpleasant to her.

Ergo, Stephanie Talcott must have regarded her as competition.

And if a woman as drop-dead gorgeous as Stephanie Talcott regarded her as competition, then Royce had deduced that—

Let's just say my vision of Julia Kendricks is getting clearer all the time.

Julia felt herself flush. Her breath seemed to solidify somewhere between her lungs and her lips. She opened her mouth to say something. Anything. She closed it again when she realized she couldn't speak.

Royce lifted his right hand and traced the curve of her left cheek. "You're blushing," he said softly.

"H-how—?" She could barely choke the word out.

"I can feel the heat." He toyed with the black pearl that dangled from her earlobe for a few mind-blowing moments, then eased his fingers down, feathering them against her sensitized flesh.

Julia began to tremble. Tiny sparks of pleasure danced along the nerve endings just beneath her skin.

"Your pulse is very fast," he murmured. The caressing sound of his dark velvet voice made it race even more quickly.

"Royce." She drew a shaky breath. "Please."

"Please, what?"

Julia swallowed convulsively, conscious of a tightening in her breasts. "I d-don't . . . I don't know."

She watched Royce's mobile lips quirk and part and she saw his even teeth sparkle. She felt him stroke his hand down the side of her neck, his fingers curling gently to touch her nape, the faintly callused ball of his thumb coming to rest on the upper edge of her collarbone.

"You know I want to kiss you, don't you?" he asked huskily.

Julia's vision blurred. Yes, of course she knew. She knew—oh, dear God, how she knew!—what men wanted to do with her. And to her. She knew what men wanted her to do with them and to them, as well. She wasn't innocent. She wasn't ignorant. She wasn't—

"Julia?"

She blinked. Once. Twice. Three times. Suddenly the world snapped into crystalline focus.

That's when she saw him. Really, truly saw him.

Not "men."

Him.

One man. Unique. Individual.

One man named Royce Archer Williams. A man unlike any other she had ever known...would ever know.

Then, abruptly, she saw herself. Her image, reflected back at her in the convex surfaces of his dark, mirrored lenses.

Julia Kendricks had spent years defining herself in terms of what she wasn't. In the space of a single heartbeat it dawned on her that she had little or no idea of what she *was.* Of who she was.

"Julia?" Royce's voice turned insistent. So did his touch. "What's wrong?"

"Nothing," Julia answered. It wasn't a lie. Then again, she could just as easily have answered "everything." That wouldn't have been a lie, either. She inhaled deeply, trying to understand what was happening to her. An impulse seized her. She surrendered to it. "Take off your sunglasses, Royce."

"Julia—"

"I know," she interrupted, stoppering his lips with her fingers. She felt him shudder at the contact and experienced a sweet thrill of feminine power. "I know what you

want. I—I want it, too. What I *don't* want is to stare at my
reflection when you...when we—"

Royce's left hand came up.

The sunglasses came off.

Royce's left hand went down.

The sunglasses dropped to the foyer's hardwood floor.

A moment later Julia was in his arms.

"You could have closed your eyes," Royce whispered,
brushing his mouth lightly over hers.

"I need to see you," she responded. She brought her arms
up and encircled his neck. "I n-need—"

"I know."

He didn't, of course. Unaware of who she was, of how
she'd once lived, there was no way Royce Archer Williams
could know the truth about what Julia Kendricks wanted.
But that didn't seem to matter during the hot, honeyed moments that followed.

The kiss was an act of courtship, not claiming. Of tenderness, not taking. Mouths melded. Breaths merged. Bod-
ies moved in an ancient and evocative partnership.

There was no separating him from her or her from him.
There was only a seamless, sensual sharing.

Julia could feel Royce's arousal throbbing against her,
bold and blatant. She wasn't afraid. She was excited. And
she was conscious of the shimmering force of her own desires, too. Desires she'd long denied. Desires she'd just discovered. Desires she'd never dreamed existed.

Yes, she thought.

Oh, yes. *Please...*

And then, without warning, it was over.

"Enough," Royce growled, breaking the kiss.

"W-what?" Julia stammered bewilderedly.

"Enough," he repeated, his voice harsh. Gripping her
upper arms, he eased her away from him. "We have to
stop."

She stared at him, unable to accept that he meant what he
was saying. His cheeks were flushed, his mouth drawn tight.
His sightless eyes glittered with a hunger that stirred both
apprehension and anticipation within her.

Julia reached out to touch him. Royce stiffened as though sensing her intention, his expression warning her off. Shaken, she lowered her hand.

"Why?" Her mouth was dry, her throat tight to the point of strangulation. The single-syllable inquiry was all she could manage.

"I can't see you."

"I—I don't understand."

"Dammit, Julia!" The curse exploded out of him. "I'm *blind!* I may be blind for the rest of my life!"

Julia shook her head in a visceral act of denial. Dear Lord. Surely Royce couldn't believe that she—no. *No!* He couldn't!

"Do you think that matters to me?" she finally asked. Her voice was raw. Small wonder, considering how much she was hurting at that moment.

Royce's compelling features contorted for an instant as though he shared her pain, then hardened into an implacable mask. "No," he answered tautly. "I don't think it matters to you."

"Then why—"

"Because it matters to me."

"Royce—"

He silenced her with a gesture. "Accept it," he said, his dark eyes seeming to fix on a point somewhere beyond her. "I have."

Accept it.

It was hours later. Julia lay, alone and aching, in the ivory-and-rose bedroom that had once been Margaret Williams's favorite.

Accept it.

She had to, she realized. She had to, because sometime during the past weeks she'd fallen in love with the man who'd uttered those words.

But she couldn't for the very same reason.

Nine

That Julia chose to remain under his roof after what had happened in the foyer struck Royce as something close to a miracle. Heaven knew, he would have understood if she'd decided to pack her bags and go.

He didn't have the words to describe what the discovery that she'd stayed meant. This unnerved him. Deep in his heart he suspected he might *never* have them. This disturbed him even more....

Royce contemplated the possibility of Julia's departure for many hours after the post-concert kiss he'd ended so precipitously. He tossed and turned in his bed as his brain spun out a dozen different scenarios, each ending with "goodbye." Once he finally fell asleep, these scenarios played themselves out—again and again—in his dreams.

He didn't actually see Julia in his dreams. What he saw was himself, watching her walk away from him. He saw himself reaching out, as though trying to stop her. The look on his face made it clear that he knew the effort was futile.

Royce surfaced from restless slumber into relentless darkness. He resisted the urge to call out for Julia when he awoke. If she was gone, no amount of invoking her name was going to bring her back. If she was there but preparing to leave, there was nothing he could do to change her mind.

Unless . . .

An apology? Royce asked himself as he got out of bed and felt his way to the bathroom. Should he tell Julia he was sorry about what had—or hadn't—happened the night before?

No, he decided, stripping off his pajamas and stepping into the shower. He turned the spray on full-force and freezing. An apology wouldn't work because he wasn't at all certain he *was* sorry. If he mouthed words without meaning them, Julia would hear the hypocrisy and despise him for it.

Assuming she didn't despise him already.

All right, Royce thought a few minutes later, reaching for a towel and beginning to dry himself. No apology. What about an explanation?

Well, what about it? he challenged, tossing the towel aside and stalking into the dressing area. He couldn't explain his actions to himself! How the hell was he supposed to explain them to someone else?

Emerson had laid out a pair of corduroy slacks and a Shetland pullover for him. After a brief debate, Royce rejected these and went hunting through his recently reorganized closet and drawers for something more formal.

He was going out, he decided. With or without Julia, he was going out. To be specific, he was going back to work. It was Friday. The top staff at Williams Venture held an assessment meeting every Friday. He'd intended to monitor today's from his study, via a speaker phone, as he'd done every Friday since he'd come home from the hospital. But forget "intended." This was a new year. It was time for him to stop hiding behind technology and start tending to his business in person.

Winnowing rapidly through his wardrobe, Royce selected a charcoal gray suit, a white shirt and a burgundy tie.

He was able to identify each garment by checking the knots of thread Julia had stitched into their labels.

Royce donned a pair of cotton briefs, pulled on the wool trousers, then shrugged into the crisply ironed shirt. He was in the middle of fastening his cuffs when he froze, the true significance of the embroidered, Braille-style dots finally registering with him.

He'd spent countless hours resenting Julia because circumstances had forced him to rely on her as he'd never relied on anyone. But she hadn't wanted to be relied upon. Everything she'd ever said or done pointed to that. She'd wanted him to be able to make it on his own, without her.

She'd never intended to stay, he thought. From the moment of her arrival, she'd been laying the groundwork for her leaving.

Which was fine. Because that was what he wanted, wasn't it?

Wasn't it?

Royce realized he didn't know. Not after last night.

He'd wanted her. Not simply a compliant female body to assuage a sexual need. He'd wanted *Julia*. He'd wanted her so much he'd hurt with it.

And that was why he'd had to force himself to stop when he did. Why he'd had to end the kiss and push her away from him. *He'd had to prove to himself that he could.*

Being in control had always been vitally important to Royce. Blindness had deprived him of far more than his ability to see. It had robbed him of his sense of self-sufficiency, of his belief that he could do for himself no matter what. It had *unmanned* him.

Yet the same disability that had rendered him impotent had given him Julia. How could he describe the effect she had on him?

Could there be a permanent place in his life for her when he recovered his sight? he asked himself suddenly.

He couldn't answer that.

Could there be a permanent place in Julia's life for him?

He couldn't answer that, either.

What if...? What if he *didn't* regain his vision? Could he accept Julia as a permanent fixture in a sightless existence?

No, he thought, shaking his head. Never. The fear that pity had dictated her decision to remain with him would drive him mad.

Royce finished dressing, uncomfortably conscious that his hands were less than steady as he did so.

He walked back into his bedroom to get his cane, checking himself in midstride when he realized he had no idea where the damn thing was. He vaguely remembered flinging the cane aside the night before instead of leaning it against the nightstand next to his bed as he usually did. Beyond that . . .

Royce finally located the cane lying beside the oak-framed cheval glass that sat in the corner to the right of the bedroom door. Gripping it tightly, he rose to his feet and headed downstairs.

He'd just reached the ground floor when he heard Julia's voice. It was coming from the dining room. A second or two later he heard Emerson say something. He couldn't make out the words.

Suddenly a wave of dizziness washed over Royce. He grabbed hold of the staircase banister and clung to it. He squeezed his eyes shut. For an instant he thought he saw sparks exploding on the inside of his lids.

He opened his eyes, straining to see those bits of light again.

There was darkness. Nothing but darkness.

After several moments Royce forced himself to let go of the banister. His knees still felt unstable, his head a little woozy. Willing himself to ignore these signs of weakness, he drew himself up. Angling his cane in front of him, he tapped his way to the dining room.

He paused in the doorway, steadying himself. "Good morning," he said.

Silence. Then, from Emerson, "Good morning back to you, Royce. Sit down. I'll be bringing you some coffee in half a tick."

Royce did as he'd been bidden, tracking the sounds of the older man's movements. After a few seconds he heard the double-hinged door to the kitchen swing open, then shut.

He shifted in his seat. The faint, spring-fresh scent of Julia's perfume tickled his nostrils. He remembered breathing in her fragrance like a drug as he'd kissed her the night before. Beneath the smell of rain-washed flowers had been the musky odor of feminine arousal.

She'd wanted him, he thought fiercely. Julia had wanted him every bit as much as he'd wanted her. And if he hadn't called a halt when he did—

Stop it!

"Have you been up long?" he inquired when he thought he could trust his voice.

"A while." Julia was back to the pleasantly impersonal tone that had dominated so many of their early exchanges.

"Trouble sleeping?"

Something—a fork or spoon?—clattered against the tabletop.

"I wouldn't say that," Julia replied after a moment.

"Really?" Royce located his napkin and snapped it open. "I would."

"You had trouble sleeping last night?"

"Surprised?"

There was a pause. When Julia spoke again, her voice was husky. "Royce, please. I don't—"

The door from the kitchen swung open.

"Your coffee," Emerson announced, quite unnecessarily. "The rest of your breakfast will be coming along shortly."

Royce clamped down on the urge to tell the older man he didn't give a damn about food. What mattered to him was what Julia had been about to say. Whatever it was, she obviously wasn't going to say it in front of Emerson.

She probably wouldn't say it once he left again, either. She'd been off balance when she'd started to speak. Emerson's interruption would give her plenty of time to recover her equilibrium.

Maybe that had been his intention, Royce speculated. Maybe Emerson's comings and goings weren't as haphazard as they seemed? Maybe he'd been lurking on the other side of the swinging door, listening?

His memory flashed back to the morning after the evening Dennis had taken Julia out to dinner. He hadn't recognized that little breakfast-time episode for what it was while it had been happening. He'd been too confused. Too angry. But now . . .

Talley O'Hara Emerson had manipulated that entire scene, Royce realized. He'd played the two of them as skillfully as the young violinist had played her instrument during last night's concert!

Royce frowned, still remembering. Well, no, he amended, not quite. As effectively as Emerson had fiddled him, his touch with Julia had been less than deft. She'd been upset when she'd left the dining room table.

Why? he asked himself. And more important, what had *really* been discussed during those fifteen minutes she'd spent in the kitchen?

Emerson's voice, brisk and businesslike, brought Royce back to the present. "Going out?" the older man inquired.

Royce's response was a single-syllable affirmative.

"Where?" The question—both worried and wary—came from Julia.

"To my office." He waited a beat. "I want you to come with me."

This is what you wanted, Julia told herself as the weekly executive meeting at Williams Venture drew to a close. You wanted to help Royce recover the life he thought he'd lost along with his sight and you have. Just look at him!

She did. Indeed, it was almost impossible for her to look at anyone else in the plushly carpeted, expensively paneled conference room.

When Royce had told her he wanted her to go to his office with him, she'd assumed that he expected her to act as his guide—as the human equivalent of a Seeing Eye dog, to borrow Stephanie Talcott's phrase—and nothing more. She'd certainly never anticipated that she'd end up seated at his right hand at a conference table!

The first thirty minutes or so of the meeting had been extremely awkward. Julia had initially thought this was due to uneasiness about Royce's blindness. But after the third or fourth time somebody had faltered while saying something innocuous like "As you can see . . ." or "From my point of view . . ." she'd begun to revise her opinion.

Royce Williams's employees were afraid of him. All of them—with the possible exception of the older woman who'd been introduced to her as Royce's private secretary, Nancy Hansen. *She* seemed impervious to everything.

As for the rest of the executive staff, well, beneath their obvious respect for Royce's intelligence and professional judgment, there was fear. Julia had too much experience with this emotion not to recognize it in others.

Royce had appeared oblivious to the atmosphere in the conference room at first. Then awareness had seemed to seep in. Julia had watched his body begin to tense. She'd seen his fingers curl inward, his back and shoulders go taut, his lips compress.

He'd cocked his head suddenly, his brow furrowing. Julia had sensed that he was listening to his employees in a way he'd never done before. She'd also sensed that he didn't like what he was hearing.

But what to do about it? Julia had felt Royce grappling with this as a chicly dressed Afro-American woman had started her presentation. She'd yearned to help him, but she'd known he had to meet the challenge himself.

"That's the conventional way of looking at the current market trend," the woman had declared dismissively after rattling off a complicated statistical analysis. "But if you look at it—" She'd broken off, her expression stricken. "Oh, Royce. I'm sorry."

"For what, Eva?" Royce had countered. "That *is* the conventional way of looking at the current market trend. And a pretty half-assed way it is, too, which is why I'm sure you're going to dazzle us with an alternative." He'd flashed a grin that had made Julia's heart skip a beat. "Am I right?"

Shifting her gaze, Julia had watched the woman stare at Royce in open astonishment. After a good ten seconds of silence, Eva's full lips had parted in a sudden, sassy smile. "Damn straight," she'd concurred.

Royce had reached up and loosened the knot of his burgundy silk tie. He'd leaned forward. It had seemed to Julia that everyone in the room—except the indomitable Ms. Hansen—had done the same.

"Show me," he'd challenged.

After that, there'd been no more awkward pauses when people used words such as "see" or "look."

"Thanks, Jerry," Royce said, addressing a burly, bearded man who'd just finished outlining the implications of several proposed changes in the federal tax code. About forty minutes had passed since the exchange with Eva. Julia watched Royce push back his left cuff and finger the face of the Braille timepiece she'd given him. The easy, open way he did it pleased her. Yet it evoked a sense of sadness in her, too. Royce's need of her was lessening with each passing minute and she knew it.

What she had to offer him was limited. Except for her newly discovered love. That was infinite. Immutable. Absolute. But given what she was—who'd she'd been—it was also impossible.

Perhaps if she'd told him the truth at the beginning...

"I think it's about time to wrap this up," Royce declared. "But before we call it quits, is Todd Reilly here? He's supposed to have the latest on the Madison bid."

The mood in the conference room changed instantly. Julia saw several people exchange uneasy glances. Several others shifted uncomfortably in their seats. She even detected a slight fissure in Ms. Hansen's stony demeanor.

"Is Todd here?" Royce repeated, an edge entering his voice.

Just then the door to the conference room swung open and a harried-looking man wearing a badly rumpled suit rushed in. He was juggling a briefcase, a dozen bulging file folders and a sheaf of computer printouts.

Everyone froze, including Julia.

"Todd?" Royce inquired into the sudden silence.

"Y-yeah," the man stammered, dumping everything down on the far end of the conference table. His face was pasty white and there were gray-blue circles of exhaustion beneath his eyes. "I'm sorry I'm late, Royce. It's good to see you—oh, *sh*—." His voice cracked. "I didn't mean—"

Royce dismissed the attempted apology with a quick gesture. Julia could tell he sensed that something was very wrong. She could also tell he wasn't sure how to deal with it.

"We can hold off on this, Todd," he finally said, obviously choosing his words with care. "Your last report was—"

"No!" Todd shook his head. "Please. I'm ready. Really."

There was a long silence. Royce broke it just before it became absolutely intolerable. "Okay," he said. "You have the floor."

Todd pulled himself together with a visible effort, then launched into what seemed to Julia to be a very cogent summation of an investment opportunity being considered by Williams Venture.

"You're satisfied with the collateralization arrangement?" Royce asked when Todd stopped speaking.

A nod of affirmation.

"Todd?"

Todd blinked several times, then obviously realized why his nonverbal response hadn't registered. "Uh, yes," he answered, his pale cheeks darkening to an ugly brickish red. "I'm sorry, Royce. I forgot you c-can't—uh, uh—"

"So do I, every morning before I open my eyes," Royce admitted with a frankness Julia knew could not be faked. "But even a blind man can see you've worked out a gilt-edged deal here. The Madison bid is a go, Todd. Draw up the papers and fast-track the financing."

"Right," Todd replied weakly, wiping his brow.

A murmur of approval went around the room.

"Anything else?" Royce asked when the reaction died down.

Although Julia could see there was, nobody said a word.

"Okay, then." Royce spread his hands. "Back to work. Todd, would you stick around for a minute?"

Although no one actually dashed to the exits, no one dilly-dallied, either. Except for Todd and Ms. Hansen. He lingered at the far end of the conference table. She stationed herself, sentrylike, at one of the doors.

Using the general hubbub for cover, Julia leaned toward Royce and asked, "Do you want me to leave?"

He turned toward her so abruptly she shrank back. "No," he said sharply. "Stay." A pause. "Please," he added in a more moderate tone.

Julia stared at him. His dark eyes seemed to bore right into her. She cleared her throat, conscious of a sudden acceleration in her pulse. "All right," she agreed.

"Good." Julia had the fleeting impression he was tempted to say more. But if he was, he overrode the urge.

Finally the number of people in the room was reduced to four.

"Still with us, Ms. Hansen?" Royce asked.

"Yes, Mr. Williams."

"Do you object to Ms. Hansen being here, Todd?"

Julia watched Todd slant a nervous look at Royce's private secretary. "No," he replied. "Of course not."

"I hope you don't mind Miss Kendricks's presence."

Todd started to shake his head, then caught himself and said, "No. Glad to meet you, Miss, uh, Kendricks. I'm Todd Reilly."

"How do you do, Mr. Reilly," Julia responded, offering him what she hoped was a reassuring smile.

"Miss Kendricks has been helping me find my way in the dark," Royce commented dryly.

"Oh?" Todd forked a hand through his desperately disheveled hair and shifted his weight from one foot to the other. "Uh, look, uh, Royce—"

"What's wrong, Todd?"

"W-wrong?"

"You sound like you're on the verge of a breakdown. I imagine you look even worse. There's obviously a problem. I'd like to know what it is." Royce's tone turned autocratic. *"Now."*

Todd swallowed hard, his Adam's apple bobbing wildly above his haphazardly knotted tie. Julia could see he was struggling against tears. A split second before she opened her mouth to intervene, he choked out, "It's my daughter."

"Your daughter?"

"Peggy. Mary M-Margaret."

Julia heard Royce inhale sharply at the middle name.

"She had an accident ten days ago," Todd continued doggedly. "We gave her a sled for Christmas and she ran it into a tree. She may not...w-walk again." He paused, his expression anguished. "My wife and I can't—Peggy's our only child. She's just s-seven."

Julia glanced at Royce. His face had lost much of the healthy color it had acquired during their daily walks. His dark eyes were fixed straight ahead. He looked like a man confronting a nightmare. She thought back to the story Dennis had told her about his defiant journey to his dying mother's bedside. Unable to stop herself, she reached out and laid her hand against Royce's forearm. If he registered her touch, he gave no sign of it.

"Is Peggy still in the hospital, Todd?" he asked after a few seconds.

"Yes."

"That's where you were before today's meeting?"

"Yes."

"And last week—"

"I set up a conference call with the hospital, Mr. Williams," Nancy Hansen cut in. "I was planning to do the same thing today."

"Only I decided to forgo the speaker phone and put in a personal appearance."

"I got here as quickly as I could," Todd said.

Royce's brows came together. "You thought being at today's meeting was more important than being with your daughter?"

Julia gasped. She withdrew her hand from Royce's arm. *How could he possibly ask...?*

"I apologize, Todd," Royce said curtly. He shook his head as though trying to clear it. "I know you don't think that. But given the way you rushed over here, you obviously think that *I* think—"

"I phoned him," Nancy Hansen cut in. "If there's any blame—"

"If there's any blame, Nancy, it's mine," Royce declared bluntly. He was still very pale. "Todd, I'm sorry about your daughter. I'm also sincerely sorry that things I've said or done made this time harder on you than it had to be." The pain in his voice was almost more than Julia could bear. She closed her eyes, berating herself for her misjudgment of a few moments ago. "I didn't understand. I didn't . . . see."

"B-but—" Julia heard Todd stammer.

"No buts," Royce cut him off. "Go back to the hospital. Be with your family. They're all that matters right now. And unless there's something you need—something the firm can do to help—I don't want to hear from you again until you've got good news about Peggy."

"What are you looking at?" Royce asked Julia about ninety minutes later. They were sitting in the back of a cab, which was sitting in the middle of a traffic jam.

"Not what," came the soft correction, "who."

"Ah." He tilted his head back. "Any conclusions?"

"A few."

"Care to share them?"

There was a pause, punctuated by the sudden blat from a car horn.

"You were very kind to Todd Reilly," Julia said, sidestepping his query.

"Making amends for a wrong has nothing to do with kindness."

"You went beyond making amends, Royce," Julia countered. "You had Ms. Hansen arrange to have Peggy moved to a private room. You called that toy store—"

"I gave orders. I spent money." Royce flexed his fingers against the slick vinyl covering of the taxi seat. "Not much of an effort in the overall scheme of things."

"You made a difference." Julia's voice was quiet but full of conviction. "Believe me."

Royce closed his eyes. Unbidden, his mind slipped back in time.

Don't, he heard a child-woman with a battered face beg him. *Please. D-don't . . . g-go.*

"Royce?"

He opened his eyes on impenetrable darkness and turned his head. "Have you ever done anything you're ashamed of?"

The question shocked his companion. He could hear it in the out-rush of her breath. He could feel it in the stiffening of her body.

"I think...everyone has," she replied after a long pause.

He almost told her. Right there, right then, he almost told Julia about the girl in the gutter, about the plea she'd made and the promise he'd broken. The confession trembled on his tongue, but he choked it back. The taste was indescribably bitter.

There was no way to explain to a woman like Julia Kendricks what he'd done or why he'd done it, he told himself. She was a woman of endless generosity. A woman whose compassionate spirit had illuminated some of the blackest moments of his life. How could he admit his indifference— his *emptiness*—to someone like her?

Royce exhaled on a long sigh, recalling how Julia had touched his arm during his post-meeting conversation with Todd Reilly. Did she have any idea how much that gentle gesture had meant? he wondered. It had been like a lifeline to a drowning man. And when she'd withdrawn it . . .

"Thank you for coming with me today, Julia," he said evenly. "*You're* the one who's made the difference."

They arrived back at the town house to the news that Stephanie Talcott had phoned to invite Royce to a dinner party at her home that evening.

"You should go," Julia said, battling down a sickening surge of an emotion she dimly recognized as jealousy.

Royce tilted his head in her direction. "Trying to get rid of me?"

"Of course not! I simply think it would do you good to get out, that's all."

"I've been out most of the day."

"That was work. This would be—" she glanced at Emerson, who'd delivered Stephanie's invitation in a remarkably uninflected voice "—play."

"You've obviously never been to one of Steffie's little soirees."

Royce's casual use of the nickname hurt. "I've never been to *anyone's* soiree. Little or otherwise," Julia said. "But I still think you should go to this one."

"What about you?"

Julia felt herself flush. "What about me?"

"What are you going to be doing while I'm out... playing?"

"Oh." She manufactured a light laugh. "I'll think of something."

"You *could* call Dennis."

"Ah, Miss Talcott mentioned something about Dr. Mitchell being invited to her dinner party, as well," Emerson inserted quickly.

Julia took a steadying breath. "Good," she said, meaning it. Although she genuinely believed accepting Stephanie Talcott's invitation would be a positive step for Royce, she recognized there were risks. Knowing that Dennis Mitchell would be on hand went a long way toward assuring her that everything would be all right.

"I don't like the idea of leaving you alone," Royce asserted.

"I won't be alone. Emerson's going to be—"

"Actually, I'm off for a long weekend," the older man interrupted, his tone apologetic. "But I'd be pleased to delay my leaving—"

"No," Julia refused immediately, trying not to think about the implications of the information she'd just heard. An entire weekend? Just her and Royce? "If anyone deserves a break, it's you, Emerson. Go. Enjoy yourself." She turned back to Royce. "You, too. Go to dinner at Stephanie Talcott's and have a good time."

Royce and Emerson left the town house about fifteen minutes apart. Emerson departed in a taxi, Royce in Dennis Mitchell's car. Julia waved them off with a smile and extremely mixed emotions.

After picking at a dinner left for her by Royce's housekeeper, Mrs. Wolfe, she retreated to her ivory-and-rose bedroom to catch up on her correspondence with the Kendricks. She wrote letters to John and Emily, Ty and Lee, then taped a message for Peter on a small cassette recorder she'd brought with her when she'd moved into Royce's house.

The letters went fairly quickly. It was easy to edit on paper—to confine herself to upbeat chitchat. The tape took much longer. She had to keep going back and erasing remarks that revealed too much about what she was feeling. There was so much she didn't want to say.

She loved Royce Williams, and she was going to leave him. Soon. Very soon.

The leaving had been a given from the start, of course. But the loving. Oh, Lord, the loving!

Julia knew she'd idealized the man who'd saved her life. Yet the ideal had never stirred her heart or soul or body. It was the man himself—the *real* Royce Williams, with all his flaws—who moved her to the very core of her being.

Sighing, Julia rewound the cassette and popped it out of the machine, then slipped it into a large envelope along with the letters. She would put it in a mailbox tomorrow, when she went out for her daily walk. Although there was a tray on a table in the foyer for outgoing letters, she'd always been wary of using it. She wanted to keep her correspondence absolutely private.

Julia glanced at her wristwatch. It was a bit past ten. She wondered fleetingly how long Stephanie Talcott's "little soiree" might last.

Smothering a yawn, Julia got up from the beautifully made antique desk at which she had been sitting and padded into the bathroom that was attached to her bedroom suite. Stripping off her clothing, she stepped into the shower and turned on the taps.

She stayed under the gushing water for a long time, soaping her body and shampooing her hair. By the time she emerged from the shower, the bathroom was as steamy as a tropical rain forest.

After toweling off and donning a flannel nightshirt, Julia began drying her hair. About midway through the job, she thought she heard something through the hum of the blow-dryer. Switching the dryer off, she listened for a few seconds. Nothing. She turned the dryer back on.

Her arms were aching by the time she finally finished. She was just about to start braiding her hair for bed when she heard a loud thud. Her heart leapt when she realized the sound had come from the other end of the hall—from Royce's room.

The door to Royce's bedroom was almost closed when Julia reached it. An instant before she pushed it open, she heard something smash against the floor. Then she heard Royce curse, his voice savage with anger.

"Please," Julia prayed, steeling herself against an instinctive shiver of fear. "Oh, please . . ."

She opened Royce's bedroom door, slowly.

She spoke his name, softly.

He turned to confront her.

Although there were no lights on in the room, the curtains on the windows had not been drawn. The moon outside was full. Its silvery glow allowed Julia to see what she needed to see.

A blotchy food stain on the front of Royce's white shirt told part of the story. The expression on his angular face told the rest.

"Oh, Royce," she whispered.

"You weren't there," he accused rawly. "I needed you, Julia. And you weren't there!"

For Julia Kendricks—once Juline Anna Fischer—there was only one possible response. "I'm here now, Royce," she said.

And then she went to the man she loved.

Ten

To touch...

The satin of her naked skin and the silk of her unbound hair.

To taste...

The intoxicating flavor of her pliant mouth.

To hear...

The quivering breathlessness of her voice when she spoke his name.

To smell...

The heady fragrance of her feminine flesh.

Royce Williams had never been as aware of another human being as he was of Julia Kendricks. He was as attuned to her responses as he was to his own. Maybe more so.

She was his haven. His helpmate. His need for her—for only her—was as immutable as it was absolute.

"Julia," he whispered against her trembling lips. "Oh, Lord. *Julia.*"

She yielded to him in an act that blended surrender and seduction in equal, erotic measure. Accepting the intrusion of his tongue with a throaty sigh, she swayed against him like a sapling in a strong wind. Royce felt himself rise in primitive response to the quicksilver allure of her supple body. Despite the layers of clothing that separated them, he was acutely aware of the press of her nipples against his chest. His fingers tingled with the urge to uncover them and the lushly rounded breasts from which they grew.

He deepened the kiss, savoring the hot, honeyed flavor that was uniquely Julia's. His breathing quickened and his muscles clenched as he felt her answer his imperative explorations by sliding her tongue lightly over his. She licked at him with delicate deliberation. The kittenlike caress sent a wild rush of pleasure surging through him. He groaned deep in his throat.

The image of a woman shimmered to life in his mind. She had fair skin, pale hair and beautiful, blue-green eyes. She beckoned to him, smiling. The graceful movement of her slender-fingered hands and the slow curving of her lovely mouth were rich with promise. Royce's heart leapt in recognition.

He tried desperately to sustain the picture—to claim it for his own and fix it in his brain for all time. But the greater the effort he made, the less focused his vision became. The exquisite image dissolved like a dream, leaving him engulfed in darkness once again.

From somewhere deep within that lightless void he heard the haunting echo of a decade-old plea. *Don't. Please. D-don't... g-go.*

A moment later Julia said his name. Her voice seemed to reach him across a great distance. Then he felt the soothing flow of her palms up his spine and the butterfly light brush of her lips against his own.

If her intention was to rouse him from the past and rivet him to the present, she more than achieved her end. Yet there was a curious quality of absolution in her touch, as well.

Royce slid his right hand inward from the curve of her shoulder, his fingers winnowing through the luxurious disorder of her hair to clasp the back of her neck. He caressed the soft skin of her nape as his left hand stroked down her back. Flattening his palm at the base of her spine, he drew her hard against him. He claimed her mouth in an ardent, impassioned caress. Nothing he had done before had ever seemed as right.

Julia exhaled on a shattered gasp when Royce finally lifted his lips from hers. His own lungs were laboring for air. Every breath he took was redolent of the scent of her hair and skin. The pungently provocative fragrance hazed his brain.

They kissed again, mouths moist and malleable. Their tongues toyed and intertwined. The taste of her became the taste of him, and the blending was as addictive as a drug.

"Please." Julia sounded dizzy. Even a little desperate. "Oh . . . p-please."

"Anything," Royce pledged fervently, feeling for the buttons he'd detected on the front of whatever it was she was wearing. The thickness of the fabric from which the long-sleeved, high-necked garment was made—what was it, flannel? Double-ply cotton?—was a frustration. He wanted Julia in something sleek and sheer and easy to slip off.

Better yet, he wanted her in nothing but a sheen of perspiration and a hot-blooded blush.

One small, slick-surfaced button succumbed to his less-than-deft efforts to undo it.

A second followed.

Then a third.

And after several nerve-shredding seconds of fumbling, a fourth.

Royce's hands were shaking. Drawing hard on a rapidly draining reservoir of self-discipline, he schooled them into steadiness. Then, carefully, he sought and found Julia's newly bared breasts.

Had she been created expressly for him, she could not have fit his palms more perfectly. He cupped the soft weight of her firm yet fragile flesh gently, his fingers curving in slow, sensual possession.

"Beautiful," he murmured, absorbing the full implications of the word he'd never before applied to something he couldn't see. "So . . . beautiful."

Julia's nipples stiffened in answer to his questing touch, going from pouting buds to thorn-stiff peaks in the space of a few hammering heartbeats. The areolae that circled the changeable nubbins of flesh were transformed by his tactile attentions, as well—smooth as a rose petal one moment, pebbled like cut velvet the next.

It was all new to him. Every texture was fresh. Every response, tantalizingly unfamiliar. The past was useless as a frame of reference. What Royce Williams was experiencing was profoundly different from anything he'd ever known.

And it was new to the woman in his arms, as well. He could feel it in the way she shuddered at his touch, as though the intensity of her physical reactions kept catching her by surprise. He could hear the same message of startled wonderment in the increasingly erratic pattern of her breathing. He sensed that whatever expectations Julia Kendricks had brought to this encounter—expectations about him, about herself, about the two of them together—they'd long since been overtaken by the white-hot exigencies of what was actually occurring.

"Royce," Julia whispered raggedly, her warm breath fanning across his mouth. "Oh, Royce."

He felt her begin to unfasten the front of his shirt. Despite her advantage of sight, her efforts at unbuttoning seemed almost as clumsy as his had been. Finally she tugged the garment free of his trousers and peeled it away from his torso. There was a brief stir of cool air against his skin, followed by the warm glide of her hands.

A growl of pleasure clawed its way up from Royce's chest as Julia charted him with her palms and fingers. The growl became a groan of something close to pain when she found the tightly furled buttons of his masculine nipples.

Nails traced teasingly over the nerve-rich knots of flesh. Royce shook like a man in the grip of a fever. Streaks of heat spiraled through his nervous system.

Lips nuzzled languidly where nails had so delicately tormented. Teeth nibbled at him with exquisitely calibrated control. The spiraling streaks of heat ignited a wildfire that damn near incinerated him.

His shirt came off. So, too, the ungainly garment Julia had been wearing. A moment later he felt her knuckles graze his belly. He sucked in his breath, the muscles of his lower body contracting in violent, involuntary response to the contact. A moment after that he felt her start to undo the buckle of his belt.

Royce's body was taut with anticipation long before Julia finished undressing him. The clamor in his blood was peremptory. It pulsed from his temples to his toes, pounding out its demands most insistently in the blunt rod of flesh between his thighs.

He was never entirely certain how the two of them got to his bed. Logic argued that Julia must have led him there. Yet a sensation-blurred memory suggested she'd made the short but decisive journey in his arms, guiding him to their mutually desired destination with a few breathlessly whispered words.

To feel...

The lushness of her body as she lay beneath him, the jewel-hard tips of her breasts brushing his chest.

To taste...

The plundered sweetness of her lips. The salty tang of her throat and shoulders.

To hear...

The cry of pleasure as he stroked his fingers against the petaled flesh that marked the passage to the fertile secrets of her femininity.

To smell...

The primitive perfume of a need that was as powerful as his own.

Julia Kendricks excited Royce Williams as no other woman had ever done. She enthralled him in a way that, in all his adult years of detached and seemingly self-sufficient living, he'd never dreamed possible.

"Royce," she entreated. "Please. Oh, *please...*"

He did not need to be urged.

Shifting his weight, Royce poised himself against the soft heat he had tested with his fingertips only moments before. After drawing a shuddery breath, he drove forward and buried himself as deeply in Julia's yielding warmth as he could.

She was tight. Tight, but not untried. That small but significant fact burned its way into his consciousness a throbbing instant before he realized the body beneath his had gone rigid.

The darkness that enveloped him suddenly turned oppressive. It was not that Royce had forgotten he was blind. He could never forget that. But in the past few minutes his other senses had inundated him with such splendor that his lack of sight had seemed less of a deprivation. As a result, his renewed awareness of his disability impacted on him with an especially bitter force.

"Julia?" he asked hoarsely. "Julia, what—"

Royce heard a whimper. The sound was soft and small and shattered. There was no mistaking its source.

Comprehension descended like a cudgel.

He'd hurt her.

Dear heaven.

He'd hurt her.

He levered himself up, ready to abandon what his thoroughly primed body was screaming was the swift, sure path to paradise. He was cursing under his breath. The sense of self-loathing he'd experienced in the aftermath of Stephanie Talcott's dinner party returned full-force, washing over him like a toxic wave.

"Don't!"

The unequivocal syllable was underscored by the bite of Julia's nails. Royce welcomed the stinging dig as the beginning of penance for what he'd done.

He'd thought he'd changed since her arrival. He'd honestly believed he'd spent the past four weeks learning to "see" other people instead of focusing exclusively on himself. How wrong he'd been! Julia's pain, the pain he had caused in his heedless rush toward his own selfish pleasure, testified to the depth of his misjudgment.

"I have to," he rasped, trying to ease back and away, trying to keep his movements gentle. "I'm hurting you—"

"Hurting m-me?" Her shaky voice was dulcet with disbelief and something that sounded bizarrely close to laughter. "No, you aren't. You c-couldn't."

"But I can feel—"

"So—" a sudden shudder *"—can I!"*

The body beneath Royce's was no longer rigid. A moment after his bewildered brain managed to accept this truth, he felt Julia begin to shift against him. She arched up, reclaiming the hard length he'd partially withdrawn from her liquid core. He groaned as she took him into herself with a movement that was both greedy and giving.

It had taken every shred of willpower he had to drag himself away from the brink of fulfillment. Julia drew him back to the edge of ecstasy with a languid tilt of her pelvis. She would have sent him tumbling over had he not seized control of a nearly uncontrollable situation with his own two hands.

"Wait," he pleaded through gritted teeth, struggling against the conviction that some portion of his anatomy was about to explode. He gripped Julia tightly, trying to keep her quiescent while the urgency of his need abated just a little. "Please. Wait."

She did as he asked. But only for a few seconds.

It was long enough.

Royce adjusted his hold, his palms slipped over Julia's hips and under her bottom. He lifted her to meet his downthrust, sheathing himself in her velvety heat with a gliding, sliding stroke.

"Oh..."

"...Yes."

He felt the first tiny ripples that signaled the start of his new lover's release less than a second later. He reached the outermost limits of his self-restraint barely a second after that.

And as the world shattered apart and rationality unraveled, each found the key to completion in the other.

It was only afterward—after the fever in his blood had cooled and his heartbeat had slowed to something approaching normal, after Julia had fallen asleep within the circle of his arms—that Royce asked himself the inevitable question.

Why?

Why had Julia done it? Why had she made love with him on this, of all nights?

He lay in the darkness that seemed to define so much of his world for an unknowable length of time, examining reasons and exploring motives. In the end, he eliminated all the possibilities but one.

Julia stirred. Royce instinctively tightened his hold on her. She stirred a second time, murmuring something beneath her breath as she snuggled closer. A moment later he felt the nuzzle of her lips against his chest. He stiffened, trying to stifle a groan.

Why had she done it?

The answer to the inevitable question was obvious to him. It was also completely unacceptable.

Julia surfaced from a state of deep, dreamless slumber into a silent, softly lighted world that didn't seem quite real—or quite right. There was an unfamiliar tenderness in her breasts and an odd throbbing between her thighs. The stir of the fine-loomed cotton sheets against her bare skin sent tiny shivers—

Bare skin?

Julia experienced a heart-stopping moment of panic as she realized she was alone and naked in a bed that carried the musky, unmistakable odor of sex. Her mouth went dry and her throat closed up as a sense of déjà vu that dated back more than a decade threatened to devastate her.

And then she remembered. She remembered everything.

The explicit kisses.

The intimate caresses.

The ineffable sense of consummation.

Julia sat up, her hair streaming over her shoulders and down her back. "Royce," she whispered, old fears receding as a flood of recently minted memories rushed in to take their place. Her heart began to beat again and she recovered the ability to breathe. *"Royce."*

She closed her eyes for a moment, embracing the sensations that were sweeping through her instead of trying to escape them.

Julia Kendricks—aka Juline Anna Fischer—had no frame of reference by which to judge the ecstasy she'd discovered in Royce Archer Williams's arms the night before. It was beyond the scope of her experience or her imagination. All she knew was that the act that had always seemed so shameful to her had been transformed into a shimmering source of splendor. For the first time in her life she felt as though she was—

"Julia?"

She opened her eyes, every fiber of her body quivering with awareness.

Royce had materialized in the doorway that led to the dressing room. He was clad in a knee-skimming robe of burgundy-and-navy paisley silk that emphasized the width of his shoulders and the leanly muscled power of his torso. His dark hair was slicked back from his face, underscoring the virile angularity of his features.

A surge of yearning washed through Julia. Her mouth tingled with the intensity of the emotion. Her nipples contracted as though anticipating an expertly erotic touch. She pressed her thighs together, triggering a wild fluttering deep inside her belly.

She felt herself begin to blush. Succumbing to some ancient impulse toward modesty, she lifted a corner of the badly rumpled bedsheet and brought it up to cover her breasts. She knew the gesture was absurd, given the circumstances, but she couldn't stop herself from making it.

"Good morning," she finally managed.

Royce cocked his head as though homing in on the sound of her voice. "If you say so," he answered flatly.

Julia shifted, a sudden frisson of uncertainty skittering up her spine. "Don't you?" she asked after a moment.

The bedroom's main window was fitted with a cushioned seat. Royce crossed to it in a few lithe strides and, after a fractional hesitation during which he verified his location by touch, sat down. "I'll concede the morning part," he said as he settled himself.

"But not the good?" Julia moistened her lips.

Royce shrugged, seemingly indifferent, then averted his face. The gray strands at his temples glinted silver in the early morning sunshine. The small muscles along his strong jaw bunched and released. His sensually shaped lips thinned into an expression that suggested endurance.

There was an unpleasant pause. Finally, Julia slid out of bed. She tugged the sheet free as she did so, wrapping it around herself. Then, slowly, she walked toward the window seat.

She came to a halt just within touching distance. She drew a deep breath, trying to steady herself. The love she felt for Royce Williams endowed her a special kind of strength. Yet it also deprived her of most of the emotional defenses she'd built up over the years.

"Royce?" she asked.

No response. He was as still and silent as a statue.

"Please." She reached out with her right hand. "Tell me what's—"

Although she only brushed her fingertips against his robe-covered shoulder, Royce reacted as though she'd burned him to the bone. He turned on her with such abruptness that Julia actually fell back a step, nearly stumbling on the trailing end of the sheet as she did so.

"There's nothing to tell," he said harshly.

"But—"

"I'm fine, Julia. Isn't that what you want to hear?"

"No!" she denied. "Not when I can see it isn't true!"

Her lover of one night sucked in his breath as though she'd slapped him. Then, astonishingly, the stony set of his features began to crack. Julia clasped her hands together as she watched Royce's expression go from implacable to deeply, almost desperately vulnerable.

A split second before the silence became completely unbearable, he asked, "Why did you go to bed with me?"

Because I love you, her heart answered instantly, offering the ultimate, immutable truth.

"Because I wanted you," she replied aloud several seconds later, retreating to a fragmentary form of honesty.

"You walked in on a food-stained blind man having a temper tantrum and were overcome by passion?" The question was bitterly sarcastic. But beneath the sarcasm, Julia heard fear. Suddenly the reason for Royce's behavior became painfully clear to her. He was afraid she'd given herself to him out of pity!

But how could he possibly think...? Didn't he realize...?

No. Of course not. How could he?

"When I came into your room last night, I could see you were hurting," Julia acknowledged slowly. "I wanted to help you." She paused, remembering. When she resumed speaking, her voice was husky. "But the m-moment you took me into your arms, the moment you began to *touch* m-me—"

She had to stop. How was she supposed to describe the indescribable? she wondered wildly. How was she supposed to articulate the essence of an experience that had fundamentally altered her perception of herself as a woman?

"What, Julia?" Royce leaned forward. "When I began to touch you, *what?*"

"Don't you know?" It was a cry from the very core of her soul. Julia blinked against a sudden threat of tears, then forced herself to go on. "Couldn't you tell, Royce? You took me into your arms and I melted! You touched me and I c-came apart! I never thought I c-could, I mean, I'd n-never f-felt—"

She stopped a second time, her throat tight, her temples throbbing. She stared at the man sitting before her. He looked stunned, as though he was struggling to make sense of the admission she'd just made. Finally he spoke.

"You've had...other men."

It wasn't an accusation. Yet deep down, Julia realized it could have been. If Royce ever learned the ugly truth about her past...

That wasn't going to happen. Although there had been times during the past few days when she'd seriously considered confessing all, she knew last night had closed off that option for good. It had been Julia Kendricks who'd made love with Royce Williams, not Juline Fischer. To admit to Juline's existence now, after the fact—Lord, she couldn't! She simply couldn't!

"And you've had other women," she observed after several long moments.

"Julia—"

"Did you ever ask any of *them* why they went to bed with you?"

The question clearly startled Royce. Small wonder. It startled Julia, as well. Half of her wanted to recall the query. The other half was desperate to know the answer.

"Did I ever ask...?" he began in an odd voice. Julia saw series of emotions she couldn't identify streak across his face. Eventually he shook his head and said, "No. I never did. I never even thought about it." He shook his head a second time. "It didn't *matter* with them."

Julia ran her tongue over her lips. "But it does with m-me?"

Royce looked at her, his sightless gaze unfocused but intense. After a few seconds he gave her back the words she flung at him so precipitously a short time before. "Don't you know?"

Julia's heart skipped a beat. "No," she answered, surprised by the steadiness of her voice. "I don't, Royce. Not for sure."

There was another pause. Finally, Royce extended his right hand to her, palm up. It was a gesture of invitation as well as conciliation.

Julia couldn't move. Her entire body was trembling. Going to him last night had been one thing. To go to him now was entirely another.

"Please," he entreated.

One step forward and Julia was close enough to take the proffered hand. The clasp of Royce's fingers around hers was like the closing of an electrical connection.

A second step forward and they were practically bumping knees.

Royce drew her down into his lap, settling her against the tautly muscled wall of his chest. Julia could feel the hard length of his arousal through the heavy silk of his robe and the fine cotton of her haphazardly draped sheet. She shifted instinctively, conscious of a sudden pulsing heat between her thighs.

"Julia." The invocation of her name was half groan, half growl. A split second later Royce slid his hands down to her hips, constraining her movements much the way he'd done the night before. The pressure of his palms was possessive. He flexed his fingers once as though testing the resilience of her flesh.

A shudder of pleasure coursed through Julia. Sighing, she leaned her head against the solid curve of his shoulder.

"Feeling a little more certain?" Royce asked after a bit, his hold on her body easing into a tantalizing caress.

She made a throaty sound of affirmation. A moment later she felt the fan of his breath against her throat, followed by the brush of his lips.

"I'm sorry," he murmured, his voice hushed and husky.

Surprised by the apology, Julia eased back slightly and looked up into his face. "About what?"

"Before. The way I behaved when you woke up. I acted like an unmitiga—"

Julia lifted her right hand and sealed his mouth with her fingertips. "It's all right," she said. "I understand."

"But—"

"No buts, Royce. There were mitigating circumstances."

"I still acted like a bastard," he insisted, obviously determined to point the finger of blame at himself.

"And I still understand," she returned, equally determined to forgive and forget.

For a moment it seemed as though he might pursue the issue further. Then he apparently decided to allow himself the slack she was offering him. He smiled crookedly and gathered her close once again.

They sat together for several long moments. Julia breathed in Royce's masculine scent and listened to the steadily accelerating rhythm of his heart. She closed her eyes, savoring a bliss-promising stir of anticipation. She wanted him. She wanted him so much.

"Julia?"

"Mmm?"

"There's something I didn't think about last night. Something I should have."

The edge in his voice compelled her to open her eyes. She turned her face up toward his, anticipation now tinged with wary anxiety. "What's that?"

"Protection."

Julia blinked, her mind momentarily refusing to register the word. Then, abruptly, it slotted into place. She felt herself flush. Heard herself stammer something that made no sense at all.

"I'm healthy," Royce assured her evenly. "I've been tested. And except for last night...well, let's just say last night was the first time I haven't used a condom since I realized stupidity and selfishness aren't very appealing qualities in a bed partner."

The heat in Julia's cheeks intensified. Her breath seemed to wedge somewhere near the top of her throat.

"I'm healthy, too," she finally managed to say, struggling not to remember the multiple medical checks and years of counseling it had taken to convince her of this. She'd spent a long time believing she should be punished for the things she'd done. The psychological pain she'd undergone hadn't seemed enough. She'd kept waiting for the discovery that her experiences had left her tainted by a physical disease, as well.

"What about birth control?" Royce asked softly.

Julia stiffened. *Birth control?*

The image of a dark-haired, dark-eyed infant suddenly coalesced in her brain. Royce's child. Royce's and hers.

Oh, God.

Julia could feel the baby-that-might-be snuggling in her arms and suckling at her breasts. She could smell the fresh scent of its warm little body. She could hear the cooing cry of a pure and promising new life.

What she wouldn't give for the chance to translate this vision into reality!

The idea was so piercingly sweet, so powerfully tempting, that Julia came within a heartbeat of lying to Royce. But something—perhaps the burden of guilt she felt about the deceptions she'd already practiced—made her choke back the falsehood that had sprung so easily to the tip of her tongue.

"I—I don't—" she began awkwardly. "I mean, I haven't...that is, I'm not—"

Her lover's arms tightened around her. Julia knew he understood what she was having such difficulty saying.

"It should be all right," she went on hurriedly, counting days and calculating the well-ordered cycle of her fertility. She did her best to ignore the bitter pang of disappointment that accompanied the conclusion she reached. "I'm regular as clockwork. This isn't the time of the month—that is, well, last night was...safe."

"You can't be positive of that." It was impossible to get a fix on Royce's inflection.

"Not one hundred percent, no," she conceded. "But almost."

"Julia—"

"I'm telling you the truth, Royce!"

He seemed surprised by her vehemence. "I know that, sweetheart."

His unexpected use of the endearment, plus the tenderness of his tone, nearly undid Julia. She inhaled shakily, teetering on the brink of tears once again. "You do?"

Royce nuzzled his lips against her hair, stroking her gently with his hands. "Oh, yes," he whispered, the intensity of the response more than compensating for its lack of volume.

"H-how?" The single-syllable inquiry split as Julia felt Royce's teeth close on the lobe of her left ear. She was dimly conscious that the sheet she was supposed to be wrapped in seemed to be coming undone.

"Because I know *you*," came the murmurous reply. "Not as well as I'd like to, of course. But well enough to know...mmm..."

The rest of Royce's answer got lost in a long, languid kiss.

The rest of Julia's questions—the few that didn't dissolve in her mind like sugar in water the instant his tongue delved deeply into her mouth and his hands slid up to cover her naked breasts, that is—were overwhelmed by the rapturous joining that eventually followed.

Eleven

―――

"**Y**ou haven't asked what happened at Stephanie's dinner party," Royce observed late the next morning.

Julia's heart skipped a beat. She and Royce were out taking a leisurely stroll, soaking up some sunshine. Until this moment their conversation had been a combination of laughter-laced flirtation and inconsequential chitchat.

"I assumed you'd tell me if you wanted me to know," she answered after a few seconds, slanting a glance at her companion's strong profile.

Royce seemed to mull this response over. "Do you remember the discussion we had the day you moved in?"

"Yes." Julia paused, wondering how that particular "discussion" could possibly be linked to what had occurred at Stephanie Talcott's dinner party. "Very well."

"Then you must remember what you said you could do for me."

The linkage between the discussion and the dinner party suddenly became painfully obvious. "I said I could teach you how to avoid tripping over furniture and walking into walls," she recalled quietly.

Royce's mobile mouth twisted into a sardonic half smile. "Yes, well, judging by my performance Friday night, I need a few more lessons."

Julia was torn between the urge to offer sympathy and the understanding that to do so was to risk being rebuffed. "I take it Dennis didn't make the grade as a guide?" she finally queried, striving to keep her tone light.

"Dennis didn't even make it to dinner."

"What?"

"His service beeped him while we were walking up to Stephanie's front door. Some kind of medical emergency. He had to go to the hospital right away."

"So he just left you there?"

"I told him I could manage by myself." Royce's tone indicated that this "telling" had been unequivocal, leaving no room for argument. "Plus, Cutter Dane volunteered to drive me home."

"Oh."

"I might not have been so sanguine about the situation if I'd realized Stephanie was serving lobster."

Julia checked herself in midstride. *"Lobster?"*

"She didn't do it deliberately." Royce grimaced slightly and gave a brief rather bitter laugh. "Well, actually, she did. Steffie knows I love lobster. She was trying to please me. Unfortunately, she didn't give much consideration to the logistical problems of asking a blind man to scavenge for his supper."

Julia didn't know what to say. Her immediate impulse was to judge Stephanie Talcott a lot more harshly than Royce seemed inclined to do. How could the woman have been so thoughtless? she wondered.

"It must have been *difficult* for you," she finally commented, selecting the adjective with great care.

Her companion shrugged and took her arm. "At least I didn't have to look at the mess I made."

They resumed walking.

"I don't suppose you have any helpful hints?" Royce eventually inquired.

"Hints?"

"About the best way of handling uncracked crustaceans without the benefit of sight."

Julia smiled ruefully. "I'm afraid not. I've never eaten lobster."

"You've been deprived of one of the great pleasures of life, then."

The word "pleasures" triggered a rush of memories. Julia felt herself flush. "I wouldn't say that," she disputed, conscious of a sudden breathiness in her voice.

Royce turned his head toward her. She had the distinct impression he was picking up the sensual flavor of her thoughts and savoring it. "You will."

Julia ran her tongue over her lips and glanced questioningly at Royce. He was lolling a few feet away from her, sipping a glass of wine. Clad only in a pair of dark pajama pants—pajama pants that dipped to just below the shallow indentation of his navel—he projected an aura of indolent sensuality.

"Now what?" she asked, shoving up the sleeves of the silk robe she was wearing for the umpteenth time. The robe, which happened to be Royce's, was her only item of clothing. He'd insisted she don it in lieu of what he'd described as "that godawful flannel thing from Friday night."

"Now you suck out the rest of the good stuff," he informed her.

"I beg your pardon?"

Royce grinned roguishly and repeated himself.

Julia transferred her gaze from her lover's compelling face to the item she was supposed to suck on. "Are you sure about this?" she asked.

"Trust me, sweetheart. Even Amy Vanderbilt says it's okay to suck, provided you don't make any rude sounds."

Although Julia had heard Royce apply the word "sweetheart" to her quite a few times during the past day and a half, it still ignited a warm glow within her.

"Is it all right to use my fingers?" she questioned after several breathless seconds.

"Absolutely."

"Well, in that case..."

Frowning slightly, Julia pushed the sleeves of Royce's robe back up her arms once again. Then she used her left hand to firmly grasp the scarlet carcass of the chilled lobster she'd spent the last thirty minutes devouring under her lover's expert tutelage. She employed her right hand to twist off one of the crustacean's small claws. After dipping the body end of the claw into a bowl of delectably herbed mayonnaise that was gallantly proffered by her eating instructor, she conveyed it to her mouth.

"Good?" Royce inquired, setting down the bowl.

Julia sucked a bit too greedily and produced a juicy-sounding slurp. "Oops," she apologized, dropping the claw back onto her plate.

"Oops?"

"You said I wasn't supposed to make rude sounds."

Royce took a drink of wine. "I'd hardly classify that little, uh, whatever you just did, as a rude sound, Julia. Especially not when I compare it to some of the noises you made this morning when you, uh, hmm. Now how can I put this delicately?"

"You can't," Julia retorted, wondering if her cheeks were as red as they suddenly felt. "So don't even try. Besides, any sounds I made this morning weren't my fault."

"You're not implying they were mine, I hope?"

Julia yanked off another claw. "Not at all," she replied sweetly. "I'm saying it straight out."

"Oh, really?"

"Yes, really."

"I suppose you're going to blame me for what happened during my workout yesterday afternoon, as well?"

Julia almost choked on a shred of lobster meat. "N-no," she sputtered. "I, uh, that was, uh, I'll concede that that was my, um, suggestion."

"And a very suggestive suggestion it was, too."

"Royce—"

"I'm just grateful you didn't try to fudge the number of repetitions the way you usually do. I mean, even *my* stamina has certain—"

"*Royce!*"

"Yes?" The innocence in his voice would have done credit to an unfledged choirboy.

Julia resorted to a singularly inelegant phrase occasionally utilized by her self-designated sibling, Peter. "Stuff it."

Royce lifted his brows. "Isn't that what you were begging me to do when we were together on the exercise machine?"

She had to laugh. It was either that or smack the man with a picked-over lobster tail.

"Now *that*—" the tone was velvet-soft "—is a lovely sound."

The compliment affected Julia like a caress. "Thank you," she responded after a moment or two. Her heart was beating very quickly.

"No, sweetheart. Thank *you*."

Roughly forty-eight hours had passed since Julia Kendricks had told Royce Williams she was there for him and then demonstrated the truth of her declaration in the most intimate way imaginable. In many ways, those forty-eight hours had been the sweetest of her life. Yet in the midst of the joy they'd offered her had been the poignant awareness that her time with the man she loved was drawing inexorably to a close.

If only...

Stop it! Julia told herself fiercely. She shook her head, trying to clear it of thoughts she knew would do nothing but exacerbate the pain to come. She couldn't afford to indulge in if-only's. She had to accept what was and endure what had to be.

But it was hard. Dear Lord, it was so hard! Especially at moments like this, moments when reality seemed like the fulfillment of dreams she'd never allowed herself to have.

It had been Royce's suggestion that they have a picnic-style dinner in front of the fireplace in his study. Well, no. Not his *suggestion*. The word "suggestion" intimated she'd had some say in the matter. In point of fact, her only involvement in the arrangements Royce had made following their walk had been answering the summons of the town house's front doorbell about an hour ago and escorting a food-laden functionary from one of Boston's best restaurants into the study.

"You didn't have to do this," she'd said after the waiter had set up the feast he'd brought to Royce's exact specifications and departed, whistling, with a whopping tip in his pocket.

"No, I didn't," Royce had agreed. "But I wanted to. Now, why don't we go upstairs and get undressed for dinner?"

"*Un*dressed?"

"Slip into more comfortable attire," he'd clarified. "Only please, sweetheart. *Not* that godawful flannel thing."

Julia picked up her napkin and dabbed it against her lips. "You were right about the lobster," she said after a second or two, pushing her plate away. "It's delicious. But I really can't eat any more."

"What about dessert?" Royce countered, draining his wineglass and putting it aside. He levered himself from a sitting position. The bronze-gold light from the fireplace licked over him, emphasizing the sleek power of his body and lending an almost pagan virility to the planes and hollows of his angular face.

Julia shifted, a quiver of anticipation arrowing through her. The heavy silk of Royce's robe settled caressingly against the cleft between her upper thighs. She shifted again, her skin tingling.

"What about it?" she finally returned.

Royce felt to his left and located a medium-size, lidded container that was covered with condensation. He moved it closer to him, then carefully pried off the cover.

The container was lined with crushed ice. Cradled within this frigid layer of protection was a bowl of dark chocolate mousse garnished with snowy puffs of whipped cream and crystallized violets.

Julia sighed at the scrumptious sight.

"Madam approves?"

"Madam is tempted to fall face-first into it."

"No need for that," Royce responded, chuckling. "Do you see any spoons?"

"Ah—" Julia glanced around, spotting plenty of forks and knives. "No. But that's all right. I can go into the kitchen and—"

Royce kept her in place with a quick gesture. "I've got a better idea," he said, his mouth curving into a wicked grin. A moment later he dipped two fingers into the luscious-looking dessert and scooped out a generous dollop. He extended his hand, palm up.

The gesture sent a strange thrill racing along Julia's nervous system. She made a small, involuntary sound. "Royce—"

"Just a taste," he coaxed.

After a tiny hesitation, she scooted forward. Then she leaned in and took Royce's chocolate-coated fingers into her mouth.

Oh.

Her lashes fluttered down of their own volition as her tongue absorbed the voluptuous taste and texture of the mousse.

Oh, my.

Royce eased his fingers out from between her lips very slowly.

"Good?" she heard him ask.

Julia opened her eyes. The distance between her and Royce seemed to have shrunk. What's more, the study seemed to have gotten smaller and warmer. A *lot* warmer.

"Wonderful," she managed after a moment or two.

"More?" Royce's sightless gaze was curiously focused, his expression extremely intent.

"Yes." She swallowed, hard. "Please."

Another dip. Another dollop.

This time Royce withdrew his fingers from Julia's mouth very, *very* slowly.

"No," she protested when he moved to repeat the procedure.

"No?" he challenged, cocking a brow.

"It's my turn."

Julia's hand trembled as she scooped up a small portion of the creamy mousse and conveyed it to her lover's parted lips. A shiver of excitement raced through her as she felt the laving stroke of his tongue. The shiver escalated into a shudder when he nipped at her fingertips as she slid them out of his mouth.

"More?" she invited huskily.

"Only of you," came the provocative reply.

Her breath escaped in a rush.

Royce moved the bowl of mousse aside. Then, with almost ritualized deliberation, he reached forward and placed his hands on her knees. He slid his palms upward, slowly uncovering her upper legs.

Julia uttered his name, desire flaring deep within her as he feathered his thumbs over her naked flesh. She felt the tips of her breasts stir and stiffen. The bunched-up fabric of the robe moved between her thighs, rubbing intimately against the damp, heated evidence of her susceptibility to his touch. The silken friction triggered a spasm of pleasure.

"I have a confession to make," Royce declared softly, shifting his body as he drew her closer to him.

"A confession?" she echoed dazedly, caressing his broad, hair-whorled chest with hands that were even less steady than her voice.

"Mmm," he affirmed, locating the knotted belt at her waist and pulling it loose with a gentle tug. "As much as I enjoy desserts that are cool and sweet—" he paused to kiss her "—I prefer ones that are—" another kiss, deeper and more demanding than the first "—hot and spicy."

"You do?" The robe was being eased off her shoulders and down her arms. Julia twisted and shrugged, trying to make the task easier.

"I do."

"Then why did you order chocolate mousse?"

"Because—" Royce cupped her breasts "—it was the best the chef could whip up on such short notice."

"I— Oh—" She gasped as he teased her nipples with the edges of his nails, quickening her already stimulated senses. A wild, wanton need streaked through her. The throbbing heat between her thighs intensified. "Well, m-maybe you and I can— *Oh, Royce*—"

He and she not only could, they ecstatically did. And in the course of doing, Julia discovered that even a dessert as cool and sweet as chocolate mousse could seem hot and spicy under the right circumstances.

Twelve

They both overslept the next morning, barely managing to get up, get dressed and get downstairs before Mrs. Wolfe arrived to perform her post-weekend housekeeping duties.

If the roly-poly older woman had any inkling about what had happened since her departure on Friday, Julia saw no sign of it. Whether Mrs. Wolfe's demeanor was a matter of professional discretion or personal indifference, she couldn't tell.

"Miss Kendricks and I will be at Williams Venture all day," Royce declared as he stood by the front door of the town house, buttoning his tan trenchcoat. The deftness of his fingers drew Julia's gaze the way a magnet draws iron. Her pulse scrambled as she remembered the feel of those same long, lean fingers exploring her body.

"Yes, sir," the housekeeper answered.

"We'll be having dinner out."

"We will?" Julia asked. She'd assumed she and Royce would be dining at home. Alone. If truth be told, she'd been counting on it.

Royce cocked his head in her direction. "Do you mind?"

While the question was polite, Julia thought she detected a faint employer-to-employee edge in it. She stiffened, sensing she'd just been reminded of her "place" in the Williams's household.

"No," she replied after a moment, berating herself for her foolishness. What had happened between her and Royce during the past weekend had been magical. She'd shared— no, she'd *stolen* two enchanted days with the man she loved. Two days she didn't deserve and had never dreamed she would have. But now the magic was gone. The enchantment was over. "Of course not."

"Good." Royce nodded briefly, then shifted his attention back to the housekeeper. "As I said, Mrs. Wolfe, we'll be having dinner out so there's no need for you to cook. And don't worry about Emerson. He won't be back until tomorrow morning."

"Yes, sir."

"Thank you." He reached into the right-hand pocket of his trenchcoat and pulled out a pair of sunglasses. "Julia?"

"I'm here," she answered quietly, and handed him his cane.

While the employees of Williams Venture were infinitely more voluble than Mrs. Wolfe, Julia couldn't get a fix on whether any of them sensed a change in her relationship with Royce, either. She found her reaction to this was an unnerving combination of relief and resentment.

It wasn't that she wanted to be the target of knowing looks or speculative whispers, she told herself as she sat in the waiting area outside Royce's office while he conducted a series of confidential telephone calls. She didn't! The very idea made her skin crawl.

Nonetheless, there was a part of her that yearned for some public validation of the passion she'd succumbed to in private. A part of her that wanted to be acknowledged as...as—

As *what?* she demanded silently, tightening her grip on the magazine she'd been pretending to read. What did she want to be acknowledged as? Royce's friend? His lover? The woman he cared for above all others?

Julia bit her lower lip and closed her eyes.

Yes, she admitted painfully, that's exactly what she wanted.

But what if that happened? What if Royce openly acknowledged her as any one or all of those things? What would she do then?

Would she openly acknowledge who she really was?

Would she openly acknowledge what she'd done and how she'd lived?

Would she tell the man she loved the truth, the whole truth and nothing but the truth, and risk being rejected by him, or worse?

She shook her head. No. She couldn't! There was no way—

The sound of a carefully modulated feminine voice saying her name jerked Julia back into reality. She opened her eyes and looked up into the stonewall-steady face of Royce's private secretary.

"Yes, Ms. Hansen?" she asked, wondering how long the older woman had been standing over her. Although there was no physical resemblance, she suddenly realized the secretary reminded her of Emerson. Each possessed an aura of unswerving loyalty, of knowing much and saying very little about it.

"Are you all right, Miss Kendricks?"

"Oh, yes," Julia replied. She manufactured a smile. "I'm fine."

Ms. Hansen opened her mouth as though to challenge this assertion, then apparently decided against it. She pressed her lips together for a moment, her gaze flicking toward Royce's office then back to meet Julia's.

"Mr. Williams is off the phone," she said finally. "He's asking for you."

They had dinner at a quiet restaurant a few blocks from Williams Venture. While the ambience was elegant and the food excellent, Julia found the experience unsettling. There were several moments during the meal when she had the distinct impression that Royce was on the verge of making some sort of declaration, but he never followed through. She was eventually forced to wonder whether the signals she thought she was picking up from him were actually there or whether she was projecting her own emotional turmoil.

"Are you all right?" he asked as their server bustled away to fetch their bill.

It was the same question Nancy Hansen had put to her earlier. Julia responded with the same answer. "Oh, yes," she said. "I'm fine."

"I gather you didn't eat much."

Julia fiddled with her napkin. In point of fact, she'd only picked at her food. Their waiter had made several anxious inquiries about whether there'd been a problem with the meal. She'd sensed the show of concern was more for Royce's benefit than her own.

"I think I'm still feeling the effects of last night's lobster and chocolate mousse," she replied after a moment.

It was the most personal thing she'd said to Royce since they'd gotten out of bed that morning. For a second or two it didn't seem to register with him.

Then his expression changed. He leaned forward. "Julia—"

"Here we are," their waiter interrupted, materializing by their table once again. He placed the bill in front of Royce. "I'll pick this up as soon as you're ready."

"Thank you," Royce responded after a fractional pause, easing back in his seat. It was obvious to Julia that he didn't plan to finish whatever it was he'd started to say. She clenched her hands in her lap, struggling against a sudden surge of frustration.

"My pleasure, Mr. Williams," the waiter replied, apparently oblivious to the emotional undercurrents at the table. "We're always pleased to have you join us." After nodding politely at Julia, he moved away.

There was another pause. Finally, with her nerves stretched almost to the snapping point, Julia reached across the table and announced, "I'll get the check."

Royce stiffened. "Having dinner out was my idea."

"So was having dinner in," she immediately returned.

His brows arched. "I beg your pardon?"

"Last night."

"What does last night have to do with anything?"

Everything, she thought with a flash of pain.

"I owe you a meal," she said aloud, keeping her voice steady.

"For heaven's sake, Julia—"

"I pay my own way, Royce. I don't want to feel indebted."

He sucked in his breath as though she'd struck him. A flush spread across the taut ridge of his angled cheekbones. "To me?"

Julia swallowed, shaken by the rawness of his question. She hadn't been trying to hurt him. But she couldn't unsay what she'd said, nor could she explain what had goaded her into saying it. "To *anyone,*" she clarified.

Royce's expression turned bleakly introspective. "That's a hard way to live," he observed, his tone as flat and colorless as a pane of glass.

"Sometimes," she conceded, lowering her gaze to the check she was clutching in her right hand. "But it's the only way I know."

It was his fault, Royce told himself bitterly as he listened to Julia locking the town house's front door about thirty minutes later. It had to be. He'd said or done something he shouldn't. Or failed to say or do something he should.

He didn't know how to deal with this sort of situation. Not that he was at all certain what "this sort" of situation was. That was part of the problem. He'd been stumbling around in unfamiliar emotional territory ever since Julia's arrival. And given what had happened over the weekend—

"Julia?" he said abruptly.

"Yes?" Physically, she was seven or eight feet to his right. Psychologically, the distance that separated them seemed much, much greater.

His mouth went dry. His throat closed up.

"Yes?" she repeated.

Royce swallowed, then forced himself to speak. "I'm sorry."

A sharp break in Julia's breathing pattern betrayed her surprise. "Why?" she asked after a moment or two.

"I didn't handle things very well today."

Another pause. Then, very carefully, "'Things'?"

Royce gestured, searching for words he wasn't sure he'd ever learned to describe emotions he hadn't fully accepted as his. "During the weekend," he began, "when it was just the two of us in this house, everything was—oh, I don't know! It seemed . . . easy, Julia. It seemed *right*. But this morning, with Mrs. Wolfe, and then later at the office it was . . . I mean, it seemed—"

"Wrong?"

"No!" The denial was unhesitating. "Absolutely not! It's just that . . . that—" Royce broke off, clenching his hands, trying to control the confusion roiling within him. The darkness that enveloped him turned oppressive. He felt trapped in a way he hadn't felt in weeks. "It's so complicated!" he blurted out. "So damned complicated!"

There was a third pause, much lengthier than the previous two. Finally Royce heard the click-click of Julia's heels against the foyer's wooden floor. A moment later he felt the gentle stroke of her fingers against his right arm. His entire body tightened in response.

"I know," she told him softly, almost sadly. "Believe me, I know."

"Julia—" He wanted her. He needed her. More than that, he—

Dear Lord, was there "more than that" for him? he wondered. Was he capable of more than wanting and needing?

A month ago his answer would have been an unequivocal *no*. Assuming that he'd even thought to ask the question in the first place, which he sincerely doubted. As for his answer at this moment . . .

"There's no reason for you to apologize," Julia went on. "I didn't handle things very well today, either. It's like you said. This weekend, when it was just the two of us, everything seemed r-right." Her voice trembled on the last word. He heard her take a steadying breath. Then she continued. "But the two of us being alone, together, in this town house isn't real, Royce. At least, not the way Mrs. Wolfe or your office or the rest of the outside world are real. I—we—can't pretend that it is.''

"Not even if we want to?"

Julia made an odd sound. "We have to be honest with ourselves.''

"What about being honest with each other?''

Julia stayed silent so long, he began to think she wasn't going to answer. Finally she replied, "Sometimes that's the hardest thing of all."

Slowly he reached out and touched the exquisitely familiar contours of her face. A heartbeat or two later, she turned her cheek into his palm. He slid his hand down and back, cupping the nape of her neck. She'd worn her hair up to go into the office with him. A few stray tendrils teased across his fingers.

"Real or not," he said huskily, "it *is* just the two of us alone, together in this town house tonight.''

"I know."

Giving her every opportunity to stop him if she chose, Royce took Julia into his arms. He felt her body curve to fit his. He heard her exhale on a shuddery sigh. She was trembling. So was he.

"Make love with me," he invited.

Her assent was unspoken but unequivocal.

They were half undressed by the time they reached Julia's bedroom.

"Let me—" She broke off, moaning, as he stroked her partially bared breasts.

"Let you what?" he teased, maneuvering her in what he fervently hoped was the direction of her bed. He was feeling dizzy. Not surprising, really. Given the amount of blood that seemed to be pooling between his thighs, there was no way his brain could be receiving an adequate supply of oxygen.

"Turn on the light."

"You mean, it isn't on already?" He nibbled a path downward from Julia's left ear, finding the sensitive network of nerves at the curving juncture between neck and shoulder. "I didn't notice.''

Somehow they managed to reach her bed. Using his superior weight, Royce toppled the two of them down onto the mattress.

And onto something else, as well.

"What the—" he exclaimed as he felt a jab in the middle of his back.

"Ouch!" Julia squirmed against him. "Wait, Royce—"

There was a flurry of movement as they disentangled and sat up. A moment later Royce heard the snick of a light being switched on.

"It's a box," Julia announced after a few seconds. "And it's from—" She read the name of one of the best women's clothing shops in Boston.

Royce bit back a groan of comprehension. He'd forgotten. Dammit, he'd completely forgotten about the telephone call he'd made earlier in the day! Buying Julia a gift had seemed like such a good idea at the time. But now...

"It's addressed to me," Julia added slowly.

"You should be the one to open it, then," he replied, striving for a casual tone. He knew he had to play the scene through.

"Why don't you save me the trouble and tell me what's inside?" she countered. The wariness he'd heard in the foyer was back in her voice. But there was something else. Something he couldn't quite get a fix on.

"Because I only know what it's *supposed* to be, Julia," he answered bluntly. "I ordered it *blind*."

"When?"

Royce knew she was studying him. He could feel the weight of her gaze. He raked a hand back through his hair. "I called from the office."

"Your 'confidential' business?"

"I had an impulse." He grimaced. "I gave in to it."

There was a pause. After a good ten seconds, Royce heard Julia pick up the box. He listened intently to the sounds that followed, conjuring up mental images of the actions that went with them.

The lifting of the lid.

The crinkle-crackle rustle of tissue paper being pushed aside.

Finally, a gasp of very feminine astonishment.

"Oh." Julia sounded stunned. "Oh, *Royce*. I've never seen anything so lovely," she admitted. Instinct told Royce what her next words would be. Instinct also told him how to preempt them. "But I can't—"

He held up a hand like a traffic cop, cutting her off. "Before you tell me I shouldn't have, or that you can't accept this because you don't want to feel indebted, there's something you need to know. What's in that box isn't really for you."

"It's not?"

"No. I ordered it for me."

She cleared her throat. "You ordered a shell pink, silk nightgown for *yourself?*"

He cocked a brow. "You have a problem with that?"

"Oh, no. Of course not." Her denial was edged with laughter. Royce experienced a profound sense of relief. "It's just that, um . . . well, I don't think it's going to fit."

"Really?" He had to fight to keep from smiling.

"Your shoulders seem a *little* broad for a size eight."

"Ah." Shifting his weight, Royce reached out for Julia. Palms curved, he slid his hands slowly up her arms. "Yours seem just perfect."

She stiffened, seeming to resist his touch. "Royce—"

"Shh." He cupped her shoulders, massaging gently. "All right. Yes, the nightgown is a gift. But there are no strings attached, Julia. Please, believe me. And it really is as much for me as it is for you."

"How?" He sensed she wanted to accept his word, but wasn't quite ready to trust.

"You know my opinion of that nightshirt of yours."

"You mean the 'godawful flannel thing'?"

"Exactly," he affirmed. "Now, getting you out of that and into my robe was an improvement. But, uh—"

"You want your robe back?" she suggested dryly, some of the tension easing out of her body.

"Eventually."

"It's a little worse for wear, you realize."

He chuckled. "Yes, well, I'm sure Emerson knows a discreet dry cleaner who knows how to deal with chocolate mousse stains."

There was yet another pause. Lifting his hands from Julia's slender shoulders, Royce waited it through with a patience he hadn't realized he possessed.

"Royce?" she said finally.

"Yes?" He tried not to sound too eager.

"Do you want me to put the nightgown on?"

He exhaled on a long, controlled breath. "Very much."

Ignoring the anticipatory pounding of his pulse, Royce tracked the subtle sounds of Julia's disrobing. A series of erotic images played through his brain as he listened. The graceful movements of her slender-fingered hands as she unbuttoned, unsnapped, unzipped and slipped off. The sleek curves of her hips. The elegant swell of her creamy-skinned bottom. The provocative lift of her petal-tipped breasts as she raised her arms to—

"Done," Julia announced throatily.

The images vanished, leaving behind a yearning more powerful than any Royce had ever experienced. He had to see her, he thought. He *had* to!

And then an idea came to him. Suddenly. Like a lightning bolt.

There was a way, he thought. But it all depended on her. Like so many other things in his life seemed to, it all depended on her.

"Royce?" Julia prompted, audibly uneasy. Royce knew she must be responding to the expression on his face. He could only imagine what that expression must be.

He drew a deep breath, fixing his eyes on the spot where he thought she was standing. "I need your help," he said simply.

"This—" Julia shifted her weight in a restive movement, conscious of the provocative feel of silk against bare skin "—is very difficult for me."

"Why?" Royce placed his palms beneath her jaw and gently coaxed her to face forward. They were standing in front of the oak-framed cheval glass that occupied the corner to the right of his bedroom door. She was directly in front of the mirror. He was just a few inches behind her.

"I told you. I don't like looking at myself."

Royce nuzzled his mouth against her hair. "*I'm* the one who's looking," he reminded her. "Be my eyes, sweetheart. Tell me what I'm seeing."

There was a long silence. Julia forced herself to study her reflection. Royce's instruction reverberated through her brain.

Tell me what I'm seeing.

Dear Lord! she thought. How could she tell him, when she couldn't tell herself?

Her initial reaction to Royce's request had been shock. She'd flushed, hot blood storming up into her face, making her burn from breastbone to brow. A moment or two later the blood had drained away, leaving her feeling as though she might swoon.

"W-why?" she'd finally stammered.

"Because I want to see you, Julia. I want that more than anything."

Royce had had no idea what he'd been asking of her, of course. But she had. God help her, she'd known exactly what his request entailed.

It was one thing for her to abandon her defenses against the man she loved as she'd done Friday night when she'd walked into his arms and offered herself, body and soul. It was something else entirely for her to abandon her defenses against herself, against the past she never stopped fearing would rise up and swallow her whole.

"Julia?"

She took a deep breath, still staring into the mirror. She had to do this, she told herself. Somehow, some way, she had to do it.

"You're seeing a blonde," she said quietly.

One corner of Royce's mouth kicked up, his pleasure obvious. "How blond?"

"Very." She paused, expanding the focus of her gaze to include both of them. The contrast between his dark masculinity and her fair femininity stirred her at a very elemental level, reminding her of the age-old cliché about opposites attracting. She moistened her lips. When she resumed speaking, her words were more husky than hushed. "Especially next to you."

The remark clearly caught Royce by surprise. "I hadn't thought about that," he murmured, kissing her shoulder. The caress sent a shiver of pleasure racing along Julia's nerve endings.

"Hadn't thought of what?" she asked after a few seconds.

He lifted his head and smiled directly into the mirror. The curve of his flexible mouth was extremely male. "That while you were looking at yourself for me, you might also be looking at me for yourself."

"O-oh." It was more an involuntary exhalation than a word.

"I like the idea of your looking," he went on, moving his hands over her shoulders and down her arms. "I like it very, very much."

Royce slid his hands forward as he spoke, his palms pressed flat, his fingers splayed across the plane of her stomach. Muscles deep within her contracted at his gliding touch.

She arched her back, rocking her hips. Royce's hold tightened and he drew her closer to him. She invoked his name on a ragged breath, acutely conscious of the rampant thrust of his masculinity.

Slowly, Royce stroked upward from her belly. Julia bit her lip as he cupped her breasts. Her nipples rose between his fingers, pouting against the shimmering fabric of the nightgown as though demanding his attention.

"So responsive," Royce murmured, toying and teasing until a throttled groan broke from her lips. He smiled as he had before. "You like that, don't you?" he asked rhetorically, continuing his caresses.

Julia watched her face contort for an instant as the sensations he was evoking became so intense they verged on pain. Yet she found nothing ugly in the spasming change of her expression. Just the opposite, in fact.

The bodice of the nightgown was held closed by a row of dainty pearl buttons. Royce undid them with sensuous deliberation, then peeled back the garment to reveal her breasts.

"Do you know what it does to me, Julia?" he demanded huskily. "To feel you respond to me the way you do? To feel these—" he feathered the pads of his thumbs against her nipples "—change beneath my fingers?"

His words went through Julia like heat lightning. She tried to speak but couldn't.

"They're like rosebuds," Royce went on. "That's what I picture in my mind when I touch them. Are they pink?"

"Y-yes," she managed after a few moments.

"The same pink as your lips?"

It took every shred of willpower Julia possessed to shift her gaze upward. She'd never given much thought to the color of her mouth. "Almost."

"Almost?"

Her gaze dropped. She stared at her mirrored image, conscious of a strange thrill of discovery. "Your touching makes them . . . darker."

Royce slid his right hand from her breasts to the silk-veiled cleft between her thighs. His fingers curved inward, tracing her sensitized feminine flesh through the sleek fabric of her nightgown.

"And this pink?" he asked after several shuddering seconds.

"I . . . oh, R-Royce. *Oh.* I . . . d-don't . . . know."

Julia's breath hissed out from between clenched teeth as he continued to stroke her. His touch became more and more explicit. Her legs started to tremble. She shifted reflexively, trying to increase the pressure of his fingers. Her lashes fluttered down.

Eventually, Royce withdrew his hand. "Tell me about your eyes."

"My eyes?" Julia struggled to refocus on her reflection. It blurred for an instant, then solidified again. "They're b-blue."

"Emerson said they're sea-colored. With a touch of green."

"Emerson—" she blinked several times "—described me?"

Royce nibbled at the nape of her neck, sending a rush of pleasure cascading along her spine. "Vividly."

"When...when was this?"

"The day I hired you."

"But why—?"

"Because I asked him to."

"You wanted to know what I l-looked like?"

"I wanted to know if you were as beautiful as your voice."

Julia started to turn away from the mirror. Her lover tightened his hands, gripping her in a sensual vise, keeping her where she was.

"Are you?" he questioned with velvet-voiced urgency. "Are you as beautiful as your voice?"

Julia's heart was beating very rapidly. Her blood thrummed, her body throbbed. How was she supposed to answer that? she wondered distractedly. How was she supposed to explain that the concept of "being beautiful" in any way, shape or form was utterly alien to her?

"Julia?" It was plain Royce intended to have an answer.

"Looking in the mirror like this," she began, torn between a desperate desire to tell the truth and an equally desperate fear of the consequences of doing so. "I mean, looking for *you*—" She broke off, shaking her head. Finally she confessed, "I barely recognize myself, Royce."

Royce frowned, his dark brows veeing together sharply. "Maybe..." He paused. "Maybe you've been looking at yourself the wrong way, Julia."

"M-maybe." The admission caught in her throat.

There was a long pause. Royce's eyes seemed to meet Julia's in the mirror. A strange sensation surged through her, making her feel as though she'd just made contact with a live electrical wire.

"You *are* beautiful," Royce whispered suddenly, his voice hoarse, his breath hot as it fanned across her ear. "In every possible way."

This time when she turned away from the mirror, he made no effort to stop her. Rising up on tiptoe, she locked her arms around his neck. "If I am," she said, pulling his face down for a kiss, "it's because of you."

* * *

"Julia," Royce groaned a short time later. "Oh, sweetheart."

They were together in his bed. She was completely naked. He was unclothed, but sheathed with a condom.

Julia was straddling him, her body delicately balanced. Emboldened as she'd never been in her life, she'd met and matched every one of his sexual overtures, ultimately taking the initiative with the white-hot words, *"Let me."*

Although passivity had never been, would never be, Royce Archer Williams's way, he had ceded control to her... at least temporarily. She'd exerted her sexual dominion with ardent kisses and caresses. She'd rebuffed his efforts to reciprocate with the same two syllables she'd uttered the first time she'd pushed him down against the mattress.

Let me.

The man she loved, the man she was loving, groaned again as she teased the puckered buttons of his nipples with her nails. "Oh, Julia," he exclaimed, the words erupting from somewhere deep inside his chest. "Julia. No...more."

"Much more," she countered. She stroked his torso, tracking the ripple and release of taut muscle and tough sinew, feasting on his responses with greedy relish.

Finally the impulse toward consummation became too strong to ignore. Kneeling up, Julia shifted forward, then began to take him into herself.

The merging was achieved inch by meltingly erotic inch. By the time the joining was complete, Royce's leanly molded face was flushed and she was breathing in short, sharp gasps.

He exhaled in an explosive rush, lifting his hips. Bringing his hands up, he clasped her waist. His fingers spread wide, gripping her firmly.

Julia pressed down in counterpoint to his upward thrust, moving with uninhibited grace, intuitively finding the golden mean between giving and receiving. She wanted Royce fully. Utterly. Absolutely. There was nothing she would not do for him.

"Yes..." he whispered.

"Oh, yes..." she concurred.

And then she felt them—the tiny convulsive ripples that presaged the start of her release. A guttural moan told her that Royce could feel them, as well.

She moved with increased abandon, enticing her lover toward the brink. But his discipline held a few moments longer than hers. In the same instant her control shattered, Royce reversed their positions. Rolling her beneath him, he slid his palms behind her knees, pressing until her legs flexed. He thrust forward a few hungry centimeters, his possession of her deepening, his hard male flesh stroking the throbbing nub hidden within the passion-slick petals of her feminine center.

She cried out, surrendering to him without reservation. He cried out, too, shuddering in ecstasy.

"Beautiful!" Royce gasped.

Caught up in an overwhelming force of nature, a force she realized she had helped create, Julia Kendricks believed him.

Thirteen

"Good morning, Miss Kendricks."

Julia started violently, nearly dropping the can she'd just removed from a kitchen cabinet. *"Emerson!"* she gasped, whirling around. "What are you doing here?"

The older man studied her silently for several seconds, his pale blue eyes moving from the top of her head to the tips of her bare toes. A slight quirking of his lips made Julia wish she'd donned her "godawful flannel thing" rather than Royce's exquisite pink silk nightgown before she'd come downstairs to put on a pot of coffee.

"You weren't expecting me, then?" he inquired.

Julia wondered if her face looked as flushed as it felt. "We—that is, Royce and I—knew you were coming back this morning. But, uh, it's awfully *early,* Emerson."

"I took the first shuttle flight from New York."

Julia manufactured a laugh. "Couldn't wait to get back to—"

She broke off as a muffled cry filtered into the kitchen from the direction of the foyer. The cry was followed by a thudding crash. That was succeeded by an ominous silence.

Julia dashed out of the kitchen with Emerson barely a step behind.

"The bottom line is, there's been no change in his condition," Dennis Mitchell concluded, massaging the bridge of his nose.

"It's been twelve hours!" Julia protested. She glanced at Emerson, who was standing to her right. His posture was stiff. His face, stony. Next to him was Nancy Hansen. Exactly how the secretary had learned what had happened to her employer wasn't clear to Julia, but she was thankful for the older woman's no-nonsense presence. "You must know *something!*"

"Julia—"

"Do you have any idea what it was like, Dennis?" she demanded, struggling to keep her voice under control. "Do you have any idea what I thought when I saw Royce lying there at the foot of the stairs?"

It was an image that would haunt her until the end of her days. The man she loved, sprawled in a still, silent heap. For one shattered instant she'd feared he might be dead. Then he'd groaned. The relief she'd experienced when she'd heard that sound had nearly undone her.

"I know how hard this is," Dennis assured her. "But all we can do is wait. We've determined that there are no broken bones and no apparent internal bleeding—"

"'Apparent'?" Nancy Hansen pounced on the qualifier.

"It's a possibility in a case like this." The concession was reluctant.

"Cases 'like this' being ones where the patient fails to regain consciousness?" Emerson pursued.

Dennis hesitated for a moment, then nodded.

"Royce was conscious when we found him," Julia stressed, clinging to what seemed the most hopeful sign in this horrible situation. "It was only for a few seconds, but he knew who I was. He said my name. When I took his hand, he squeezed my f-fingers...."

Her voice trailed off into silence. A pair of memories—one freshly minted and full of anguish, the other scarred over by the passage of time but still capable of giving pain—assailed her.

It's all right... help is on the way.

The words echoed across a distance of more than a decade. Words spoken by a man of wealth and privilege to a teenage runaway he had no reason to care about.

It's all right... help is on the way.

Those had been her words to the man she loved, just that morning.

A moment later Julia heard Ms. Hansen asking if she was all right. A moment after that she felt Emerson slip an arm around her.

Her answer to the question was a lie.

Her acceptance of the physical support was not a matter of choice.

"Ah, excuse me."

Julia jerked from an exhausted slump to a straight-backed sitting position in the space of a single, panicked heartbeat.

"What?" she asked anxiously, staring up at the man who'd apparently addressed her. His face seemed familiar.

"You *are* Julia Kendricks, aren't you?" the man asked.

"Yes," she replied distractedly, checking the clock on the waiting area's wall, then glancing worriedly down the corridor that led to Royce's room. Why wouldn't anyone tell her what was going on? she wondered. She'd asked and asked, but all she'd gotten was evasions. The one person likely to give her an honest answer—Dennis Mitchell—had disappeared into Royce's room along with another doctor and a nurse about forty minutes ago.

After a few moments Julia forced herself to look back at the man standing over her. She knew she knew him. But she couldn't think how. Or what his name was.

"You probably don't remember me," the man said, holding out his hand. "I'm—"

"Todd Reilly!" she exclaimed, his identity suddenly slotting into place. Getting to her feet in a less-than-steady movement, she accepted the proffered hand and shook it. "Of course. How's your little girl? Uh, Mary Margaret, isn't it? Peggy?"

"That's right," Todd confirmed with a smile. "And Peggy's better, thank you. Much better, in fact. She actually wiggled her toes Sunday."

"That's wonderful, Mr. Reilly," Julia responded sincerely, her mind flashing back to the heart-wrenching description of his daughter's condition he'd given—Lord, was it only five days ago?

"Todd, please," he urged. "And yes, it *is* wonderful. More than wonderful. It's a miracle." He paused, then cleared his throat and said, "I guess you must be here because of Royce. I spoke with Nancy Hansen this morning. She said he'd taken some kind of fall."

Julia nodded. She darted another glance down the corridor that led to Royce's room. How much longer was she going to have to wait to find out what was happening? she asked herself. Not knowing was tearing her apart!

"I think you should sit down, Miss Kendricks," Todd said firmly.

A sudden rush of wooziness made Julia decide that sitting was a very good idea. "Call me Julia," she requested, lowering herself to the sofa. "I'm sorry I'm so, uh . . ."

"I understand," Todd replied, seating himself next to her. "Believe me. I understand."

She managed a weak smile. The wave of dizziness receded.

"Are you all by yourself?" Todd asked.

"Nancy Hansen stopped by earlier on her way to work. She was here yesterday, too. For hours. Emerson—Talley Emerson, he oversees Royce's house—is around. He went down to the cafeteria to get some breakfast, I think. He should be back soon."

"I hope you've gotten something to eat, too."

The thought of food nauseated Julia. "I'm not hungry."

The look on Todd's face suggested he was tempted to lecture her about the necessity of keeping up her strength. Instead he asked, "How *is* Royce? Nancy was pretty vague about his condition."

"*Everyone* is being pretty vague," Julia stated with a flash of temper. "Royce fell down a flight of stairs yesterday morning. Since then—" She gestured helplessly.

"He's done so much for Peggy," Todd observed. His voice was soft but intense, almost as though he was being compelled to speak. "What happened last Friday was... well, it *surprised* me. I've always admired Royce Williams as a businessman. Frankly, I think he's a genius at what he does. But to tell the truth, I never really... uh—"

"Liked him?" Julia commented, recalling the impressions she'd formed during her first visit to Williams Venture.

Todd seemed taken aback by her directness. But after a few moments he nodded his head. "I suppose. In a way. It's more than that, though. The Royce Williams I saw at Friday's staff meeting was someone I didn't recognize. Now, maybe my view of him wasn't as clear as I thought it was. Or maybe I've been looking at him from the wrong—"

"Julia?"

The voice was Dennis Mitchell's. The tone was that of a man in the grip of a powerful emotion.

Julia turned, her heart pounding like a tom-tom. "Yes?"

Dennis smiled down at her. Beamed, really. Behind the lenses of his glasses, his eyes were very bright. "Royce wants to see you."

She knew his choice of words was no accident.

"Julia?"

She couldn't speak. Her heart was too full. She couldn't move, either. She could only stand there, just inside the door of Royce's dimly lighted hospital room, staring at the man to whom she owed so much and for whom she cared so passionately.

"Julia?" Royce repeated. His bed had been cranked up so he was in a sitting position rather than flat on his back. His voice, which held a familiar edge of command, was not that of an invalid.

"Yes." The one-word affirmation was all she could manage.

Royce held out his right hand. After a moment's hesitation Julia crossed to him and clasped it.

Palms kissed.

Fingers intertwined like lovers.

Julia swallowed convulsively, gazing at Royce's face, cataloging each visible injury. His lower lip was split and swollen. His left cheek was badly bruised. His right brow was bisected by a stitched-up cut that would probably leave a scar.

He looked battered. And a shade or two paler than normal. Yet all in all...

"That bad, huh?" he asked wryly, scrutinizing her just as intently as she was scrutinizing him. The warmth of his gaze was a palpable thing.

"No," Julia disputed in a throaty voice, feeling herself begin to flush. Lifting her free hand, she traced the strong line of her lover's jaw. The bristle of new beard growth sandpapered her fingers. "Not bad at all."

Royce's mouth eased into a crooked grin. "Don't try to lie, sweetheart. I've seen myself in the mirror."

Her breath caught. "Then your vision really is—"

"Well, it's not twenty-twenty," Royce interpolated, drawing her down to sit on the edge of the bed. "Then again, it wasn't twenty-twenty before I smashed my car into the embankment."

"Oh, R-Royce..." Julia was torn between laughter and tears.

"It started to come back as I was coming down the stairs. There was a flash of light. Like a camera bulb going off in front of my face."

"So that's why you fell?"

He nodded, his expression thoughtful. Julia had the impression he was trying to sort through his recollections of what had happened.

"I think I saw you for a second or two," he said slowly. "Before I passed out, I mean. You were kneeling next to me. And you took my hand and you told me it was going to be all right." He paused, his brow furrowing. "It was the strangest feeling, Julia. Almost as though I'd gone through it before. I wasn't sure what was real and what wasn't. I'd imagined seeing you so many times..."

Royce released Julia's hand and reached up to caress her face. Although his touch was gossamer light, she felt every nuance of the contact clear down to her toes.

"Emerson was right, you know," he murmured. "Your eyes *are* like the sea. Blue-green, with a sparkle of sunlight." He frowned suddenly, a shadow crossing his face. A frisson of alarm ran up Julia's spine. "They remind me of...of—"

At that moment the door to the room swung open. Julia turned, feeling as though she was trembling on the brink of disaster. She'd never considered the possibility that Royce's memory of Juline Fischer might include the color of her eyes!

"Sorry to interrupt," Dennis Mitchell apologized. "But you've got another visitor, Royce."

"Emerson?"

"In the flesh," the older man answered, stepping into view. He looked very solemn.

"It's good to see you again," Royce told him after a few seconds of emotion-charged silence. His voice wasn't completely steady.

Emerson's sober expression gave way to a genuine grin. "It's good to be seen."

Julia's sea-colored eyes filled with tears.

Her eyes were dry two days later as she stood next to the bed in the ivory-and-rose room that had been hers for a little more than a month, stuffing her belongings into a pair of suitcases. Her movements were methodical. Mechanical, even.

"You're serious, then?" Emerson demanded from the doorway, his Irish accent as pronounced as Julia had ever heard it. "You're leaving? Just like that?"

"Just like that," she confirmed, zipping one of the bags closed and tightening its leather straps with a few sharp tugs. She lifted it off the bed and set it on the floor.

"And what's Royce supposed to think when he comes home from the hospital this afternoon and finds you gone?"

Julia paused briefly, then forced herself to look at the older man. He was clutching a manila file folder in his right hand. The expression on his craggily distinguished face was grim.

"Royce hired me to help him cope with being blind." Her voice, like her movements, had a mechanical quality to it. "Now that his vision has returned—"

"That's not what I was asking," Emerson interrupted, advancing into the room. He came to a halt a few feet from the bed. *"What's the boy supposed to think?"*

It was the first time Julia had ever heard Emerson refer to his employer as "the boy." Yet the term didn't surprise her. It fit with the subtle, father-son undercurrents she'd long sensed between the two men.

"I've left a letter for him," she answered, nodding toward an envelope she'd placed on the nightstand next to the bed a short time before.

"Have you now? And how much explaining does this 'letter' of yours do?"

Julia flinched at the older man's tone but disciplined herself to sustain his gaze. "I've done what I came here to do, Emerson. There's no reason for me to stay."

"Royce's loving you isn't reason?"

The older man flung the question at her like a gauntlet. To say she was unprepared for such an inquiry was to understate the case so completely it would have been laughable under other circumstances.

Julia knew one heart-stopping instant of unadulterated joy. Then reality descended like an iron fist. She sat down on the bed so abruptly the purse-cum-tote that had been perched on the edge of the mattress fell off and hit the floor, spilling its contents.

"Royce doesn't know me," she said, denying Emerson's assertion and all it implied.

"Doesn't he?"

"No." She had to force the word out. "He doesn't."

There was a jagged pause. Julia lowered her gaze, staring numbly at the items that had tumbled out of her bag. Her wallet. A couple of pens. An address book. A handful of coins. Her airplane ticket. She was dimly aware that she was trembling.

"Tell me something," Emerson said after nearly a minute. "This letter you're leaving. How did you sign it?"

Julia lifted her head, bewildered by the question but wary of the tone. "How did I sign it?" she echoed, remembering how she'd ended her letter to Royce with the word "love," then crossed it out. "I don't understand."

"Did you write Julia . . . or *Juline?*"

For a moment Julia feared she was going to be physically ill. Her stomach heaved and a sour taste filled her mouth. Oh, God, she thought, crossing her arms in front of herself, trying not to gag. Oh, dear God in heaven.

"You . . . k-know," she finally managed to whisper, staring up at Emerson.

"I wasn't absolutely certain until just now," he replied.

"But *how?*"

Emerson suddenly looked very tired. "There was something about you. Even before you arrived. Take the way Dennis Mitchell pushed you to Royce. 'You *have* to hire her,' he kept saying. It was plain to me you had to have more than a good résumé to recommend you. Then, that first day you got here. I can't describe it exactly, but I had this *feeling.* And it kept gnawing at me. Finally I went and dug out a bunch of newspaper clippings I had tucked away." He gestured with the manila folder, then flipped it open. "They're datelined—"

"I know what they're datelined," Julia cut in. She no longer felt as though she was going to be sick. Nausea had given way to numbness. "And what they say."

A few seconds ticked by, then Emerson picked up the thread of his remarks. "There was a photograph with one of the articles," he said. "From a school yearbook, I think. Even after more than a decade, I saw a resemblance."

Julia drew a shaky breath. "If you . . . know . . . about me," she said slowly, "then you must understand why I have to leave."

Emerson's features hardened. "Never in a million years."

Something inside Julia broke. "For God's sake, Emerson! You read those articles. Don't you get it? I peddled myself on the street. I was a *whore!*"

"And Royce Williams was a poor, closed-off bastard until a month ago!" came the sharp, swift response. "Not cold or uncaring like a lot of people think. If he'd been that, if he'd been a son of a bitch like his old man, he wouldn't have needed to build so many walls between himself and the world. You broke through those walls. You got through to him—"

"*Julia Kendricks* got through to him."

"And Julia Kendricks is who you are, isn't it?"

Julia's breath caught in her throat as she remembered the reflected image of a woman with sea-colored eyes and sunshine-gilt hair. A woman Royce had called "beautiful."

She wanted to believe she was that woman. With every fiber of her being, she wanted to believe it. But she couldn't quite.

"I owe Royce Williams the greatest debt anyone can owe," she said finally. "And I've tried to repay that debt as best I could. But there's nothing more—"

"No," Emerson interrupted, shaking his head. His voice was gruff. His eyes glinted with anger. "I'll accept that a sense of obligation brought you to Royce. But I'll never believe obligation is what kept you by him these past weeks. I know the look of a woman who's with a man because she thinks she 'owes' him something, Julia. And you haven't got it. You've got the look of a woman—"

She knew what he was about to say. She also knew she couldn't bear to hear him say it. "Don't," she cut in, pleading. "Please, don't. Royce and I aren't—I mean, we could never—oh, God, Emerson. Try to understand. *I can't stay here.*"

"You're willing to leave him to go back to what he was?" the older man demanded. "Leave him to the likes of Stephanie Talcott?"

Julia winced, a pang of jealousy lancing through her. Stephanie had paid a call on Royce the day before while she and Emerson were visiting him. The redhead had breezed in bearing a huge bouquet of exotic flowers and an armful of expensive books. Her manner toward Royce had been a skillful blend of solicitousness and flirtation—part candy striper, part geisha. He had seemed amused by the performance.

"Royce sees Ms. Talcott for what she is," she said after several moments.

Frustration darkened Emerson's cheeks. "Then why don't you believe he can do the same with you?"

Royce looked back and forth between the man who'd been more of a father to him than Archer Williams had ever dreamed of being and the man who was his closest friend. Something's wrong, he thought. Something is very, very wrong.

He, Dennis Mitchell and Emerson were standing in the foyer of the town house. Royce and Dennis had arrived from the hospital only moments ago. Emerson had opened the front door before they'd had a chance to knock or ring the bell. After a quick exchange of greetings, Royce had inquired about the one person he wanted to see above all else.

Emerson's response to this inquiry had been succinct.

"What do you mean, she's not here?" Royce demanded.

"Miss Kendricks is gone," Emerson elaborated. "She packed her bags and left about four hours ago."

"I don't believe it," Royce said, clenching his fingers. "Julia wouldn't—not after we—dammit, *no!* She wouldn't walk out on me without a word!"

"Royce, please," Dennis interpolated. "You just got out of the hospital. Take it easy."

Royce's response to this unquestionably sensible counsel was an expletive. He also shrugged off the restraining hand his friend had placed on his left arm. "Emerson—"

"She left a letter for you." The older man extended an envelope Royce hadn't noticed he'd been holding.

Driven by wildly contradictory emotions, Royce seized the envelope and tore it open. He pulled out a single sheet of paper.

He stared at the page for several long moments, his brain refusing to make sense of what was written on it. The words hadn't been put down in haste, he noticed. Except for a scratch-out above the signature, the handwriting was clear and elegantly formed.

Taking a deep breath to steady himself, Royce forced himself to focus and began to read aloud.

"'Royce,'" he said. "'Thank you for everything. I owe you more than I can ever say. Please don't think leaving you is easy for me. It's not. If there was something else I could do for you, I would stay and do it. But I know there isn't. If you ever need me again—'"

Royce broke off, his vision blurring. "If I ever need her?" he echoed rawly. "*If?* Dear God, doesn't she *know?*"

There was a pause. Royce stared down at the letter, reading it over and over again, hoping against hope that the message it contained would change.

"Doesn't Julia know what?" Emerson eventually asked. His tone was careful, as though the words might bruise or break if he spoke too forcefully.

Royce lifted his gaze. He felt as though he was standing on the brink of a precipice. He had two choices. The first was to step back from the edge and revert to being the man he'd been before his car crash—the man he'd come to see with devastating clarity during the past month. The second was to step forward and embrace the man he'd been shown he had the possibility of becoming if he was willing to open his heart to the true light of life.

"Doesn't she know that I love her?" he answered simply, taking the plunge. "I love her...and I want to marry her."

There was a second pause, a lot longer than the first. Emerson finally ended it by clearing his throat and declaring in a very formal manner, "There's something you need to see, Royce. I have it upstairs. If you'll go into the study, I'll bring it to you."

If Royce hadn't succumbed to Dennis's sharp suggestion that he sit down, seeing the "something" to which Emerson had referred probably would have dropped him to his knees.

"Oh, God," he whispered when he recovered the ability to speak. His heart was thudding with the force of a hammer hitting an anvil. His breath was sawing in and out in ragged snatches. "Oh, dear God."

He fingered the yellowing edges of the newspaper articles spread before him. They were the final pieces of the puzzle he'd been trying to put together for more than a month.

Juline Fischer. The brutalized girl he'd rescued ... then abandoned.

Julia Kendricks. The beautiful woman who'd guided him out of darkness ... then left him alone in the light.

He shifted his gaze from the clippings to the letter Julia had left for him. One sentence seemed to leap off the page, its implications slicing into him like a double-edged sword.

I owe you more than I can ever say.

I owe you ...

"Payback," Royce said, the muscles of his belly tightening.

"Is that what you really think?" Emerson demanded, his voice rasping like a metal file. "Because damn you for an unworthy fool if you do."

Royce looked at the older man, stunned by the emotion he saw. While Emerson had given him disapproving glances in the past, he'd never been on the receiving end of such an angry glare.

Was that what he really thought? he asked himself. Did he truly believe the woman he'd fallen in love with had waited more than ten years for an opportunity to do unto him as he'd done unto her?

Did he?

No. No, of course not. The idea that Julia—his Julia— had come to him with the intention of offering help was consistent with everything he knew or felt about her. The idea that she'd come intending to inflict hurt was not.

"Royce?" Emerson prodded.

"No," he replied truthfully. "It's not what I think. But even so, I'm still probably a candidate for damnation." He shifted his eyes from Emerson to the clippings, to Dennis. "You knew, didn't you?"

Dennis nodded. His forehead was furrowed like corrugated cardboard. His lips were pressed into a thin, tight line.

"Why didn't you tell me?" Royce managed to temper the accusatory edge of the question.

"Because you needed help," came the uncompromising response. "And as far as I could tell Julia Kendricks was the only one who had a chance of giving it to you. All she asked in return was that I keep my mouth shut about Juline

Fischer. I would have done a lot more than that, believe me."

Royce glanced at Emerson. "Have you known from the beginning, too?"

"I wasn't positive about anything until this morning."

"You...confronted...Julia?"

The older man stiffened. "I don't want you thinking I drove her away!"

"I don't," Royce said quickly. And he didn't. His gut told him Emerson had probably tried very hard to persuade Julia to stay. It also told him the blame for her abrupt departure had to lie with him.

"Royce—" Dennis started.

"Why didn't she tell me?" Royce asked, finally giving voice to the question that had been tormenting him from the instant he'd seen the clippings Emerson had had stored away for more than a decade. "I can understand her holding back at first. But later. When I—when *we*—"

"Why didn't you tell her you loved her?" Emerson challenged.

Royce looked at the older man. "Because I only just discovered it," he answered simply. "But even if I'd realized sooner..." He paused, reliving the bitter sense of impotence that had afflicted him in the wake of his car accident. "I couldn't have said anything while I was blind. Call it pride. Or fear of being pitied. I don't know. I just couldn't."

"Do you think your being blind made a difference to her?" Dennis questioned.

Royce blinked, his mind flashing back to the second time he'd kissed Julia. He remembered the sudden surge of insecurity that had driven him to end their embrace. He'd been afraid. And ashamed. Despite the desire raging in his blood, he'd felt less than a man because of his lack of sight.

"She asked me that once," he responded, staring down at the newspaper photo of Juline Fischer. He recoiled from speculation about the forces that had driven such a fresh-faced girl onto a path that had nearly led to her death in a gutter on a cold winter's night. "Whether I thought my being unable to see mattered to her."

"What did you say?"

Royce lifted his gaze from the picture. "That I didn't think it did. But that it *did* matter to me."

"Does this matter to you?" Emerson asked, indicating the clippings.

Royce remained silent for nearly a minute, forcing himself to confront this question with absolute honesty.

"That was a lifetime ago," he finally answered, meaning it. "All that matters to me now is Julia Kendricks, the woman I fell in love with—the woman who helped me see myself and the world even when I was blind." He took a deep breath, looking from Emerson to Dennis and back again. "I have to find her. I *have* to. So, please. I'm begging. If either of you has any idea where she's gone..."

His voice trailed off. He watched the two men standing in front of his desk exchange glances.

"Julia never gave me a home address," Dennis admitted after a few seconds. "She even took back the résumé she showed me."

Frustration welled up in Royce. He did his best to quell it. "What about her final paycheck?" he asked quickly, scrambling to come up with alternative sources for information. "My medical insurance has been underwriting the cost of rehabilitative therapy. The company must have a way to forward—"

"Julia wouldn't take any money, Royce. That was part of the deal we made before I recommended her to you."

Royce exhaled on a hissing sigh. *"Damn,"* he cursed, not really surprised by his friend's revelation. "Well, then, maybe she's traceable through her family. The Kendricks. Julia talked a lot about a younger brother, Peter. She said he was blind. And a musician. He attended some sort of summer program at Julliard. That might be a starting point."

"I think you might find her—or at least these Kendricks—somewhere in southern Florida," Emerson calmly volunteered. "Julia's purse fell over while she was packing and everything spilled out, including a plane ticket. I got a look at it before she picked it up. The destination was Ft. Lauderdale."

* * *

"You're sure you're up to making this trip alone?" Emerson asked shortly before dawn the following Tuesday.

"I'm fine," Royce responded, once again calculating the time it would take him to get from Boston to the address in Boca Raton he'd received in a telephone call from a private investigator a few minutes after midnight.

"The flying is one thing," the older man said. "But you haven't been behind the wheel since the accident. You'll be in a strange rental car, driving on roads you don't—"

"I know, Emerson," Royce interrupted. "But I'll be all right."

"I'm only trying to look out for you." The intense expression in Emerson's eyes belied his uninflected tone.

"I know that, too," Royce answered solemnly. "You've always looked out for me, haven't you? But I've never once bothered to say thank you."

"There's been no need—"

"Yes, there has," Royce contradicted. "Ever since you risked your job to call me at school and tell me my mother was dying and wanted to see me, you've always been there for me. You've been there in ways I'm only starting to realize. The truth is, you've been like a father to me, Emerson."

There was a pause. Finally the older man averted his gaze slightly and said huskily, "Your mother, may she rest in peace, asked me to...to..."

"You loved her, didn't you." It wasn't a question.

Emerson hesitated for a second or two, then dipped his head in silent affirmation.

"And she loved—"

Pale blue eyes swung back to collide with dark ones. "No!" Emerson said sharply. "Your mother was a good woman. A *faithful* woman. I won't have you thinking that she and I did something shameful!"

"I wasn't judging," Royce responded, moved by the older man's passionate defense of his mother. "I mean, if you and she had been—" He gestured, trying to find the right words. Finally he said what was in his heart. "I realize her marriage to my father was a disaster. Knowing that she had you—that is, someone who truly cared for her—gives me hope she had some measure of happiness in her life."

"You were her real happiness," Emerson declared, his voice thick with emotion. "You were her treasure, boy. If she hadn't had you—"

"She would have left her husband and gone away with you."

Emerson sighed and made a weary gesture. "Her family married her off for money. Lots of it. Your father saved her father from bankruptcy and probably worse. Margaret felt the obligation every day of her married life. Maybe there would've come a time when she decided she wasn't honor bound to sacrifice herself as payment for somebody else's debt. But even if she reached that point—" he gestured again "—she knew she couldn't have me and you. Your father never would have allowed it. So she chose to stay. And so did I."

Royce grimaced. "He never had any idea, did he?"

Emerson gave a contemptuous snort. "Archer Williams was the blindest man I've ever known. He couldn't see the truth about another person—much less himself—if it was standing in front of his nose at high noon."

There was another pause. It was punctuated by the beep beep of a taxi horn, which informed Royce his ride to Logan Airport had arrived.

"Well," he said, "I have a very important plane to catch."

The older man urged him toward the front door with a quick movement of both hands. "Be off with you, then."

Royce nodded once then turned to make his exit.

"Royce—"

He pivoted back. "Yes?"

"When you see Julia, would you tell her I did what I thought was necessary?"

Royce smiled, hoping the affection and gratitude he felt came through. "I've got a better idea, Emerson. I'll bring her back to Boston and you can tell her yourself."

Fourteen

The house was a pretty pastel dwelling in a quiet neighborhood of Boca Raton. Royce surveyed the residence approvingly as he got out of his rental car, his right hand slipping into the pocket of his jacket to touch the small, velvet-covered box that had been his talisman throughout the journey from Boston. His gaze rested briefly on the mailbox by the side of the driveway. The name Kendricks was painted on it in bold block letters. He nodded to himself, sure he'd found the right place.

This certainty turned to confusion less than thirty seconds later when the front door of the house swung open in response to his imperative knock. He'd been praying Julia would be the one to answer. Instead he was confronted by two boys in their late teens. One was a tall, muscular Afro-American. The other was shorter and slimmer, with a handsome, golden-hued face and almond-shaped eyes.

"Yes?" the second young man asked.

"I'm, uh, looking for the, uh, Kendrick's residence," Royce replied, his eyes darting back and forth between the two youths. His stomach knotted with frustration. There'd been a mistake, he thought. Dammit, there'd been a mistake! These boys couldn't be—

"You've found two of 'em, man," the tall youth said, flashing a grin. "I'm Ty, the brains *and* brawn of the outfit. This is Lee. We're still trying to figure out what he's got to contribute to the proceedings."

"You've really been working on that insecurity problem, huh, bro?" Lee gibed, affection obvious beneath the sarcasm.

Royce blinked, trying to sort things out. While the names were the ones Julia had used, he'd had the impression Ty and Lee Kendricks were—

"Twins." The word just slipped out. "I thought you were twins."

Ty looked at Lee and feigned astonishment. "You mean, we *aren't?*"

"Maybe that's why you don't have a sense of rhythm," his putative brother kidded.

Ty chortled. "Give me a break. Like you can tell a downbeat from a—"

"Hey, what gives at the door?" a new voice inquired.

A moment later a slender boy who appeared to be about fifteen years of age ambled into view. Red-haired and freckled, he had a pair of hippie-style, wire-rimmed sunglasses perched on his nose. He was clad in wash-faded blue jeans and a sweatshirt emblazoned with a garish logo Royce vaguely associated with heavy-metal rock music.

He knew him. Deep in his gut, Royce knew who the boy was. He also knew why Julia had spoken of him with such tenderness.

"Peter?" he asked. "Peter...Kendricks?"

The boy cocked his head, a series of emotions sleeting across his expressive face. After a few seconds of silence he started to smile. "Yeah," he confirmed. "And you've got to be Royce Williams."

"Royce Williams?" Lee echoed, his previously cordial voice taking on an edge of hostility. "You mean this is the guy—"

"Man," Ty interrupted, his dark features hardening, his eyes flashing danger signals, "it's about time you got here!"

Royce looked at the three very different teenagers standing in front of him. "You were...expecting me?"

"Not exactly," Peter responded with a grimace. "But it's a good thing you showed up. Ty and Lee were talking about tracking you down and doing something violent."

"Me and Lee?" Ty snorted. "Seems to me like you were the one talking about whacking this dude with your cane because he made Julia cry."

Royce's heart seemed to stop. His breath wedged in his throat. "Julia's...here—?"

"It looks like somebody might have beaten you to it, though, Pete," Lee declared, ignoring the question. He eyed Royce's face with a hint of satisfaction. "I mean, this guy's got a big bruise on his cheek and a bunch of stitches on his forehead. Maybe—"

"Dammit!" Royce exploded, goaded by a desperate need. "Please. I have to know. *Is Julia here?*"

The two older teens seemed genuinely taken aback. Peter, however, appeared to take the outburst in stride. In fact, Royce had the fleeting impression the boy was pleased by his intemperance.

"She's out on the back porch," Peter responded, gesturing in the appropriate direction. "You want to see her?"

Royce breathed a silent prayer of thankfulness, then replied, "More than anything else in the world."

Julia felt Royce's presence before he spoke her name. A sense of awareness swept over her like a great wave, causing every instinct she had to snap to alert and every fiber of her body to quiver.

She turned to face him, trying to school her expression into a semblance of neutrality but realizing the task was next to impossible. She knew her heart was in her eyes.

"Royce," she whispered, clasping her hands together to forestall the urge to reach out and touch the man to whom she'd given her heart. She'd dreamed of him so many times during the seemingly endless, anguished days since she'd left Boston. Royce Archer Williams was ingrained in her thoughts and imprinted on her senses.

"You didn't really believe I'd let you go, did you, Julia?" he asked, walking out onto the porch. He stopped a short distance away from her—far enough away so she wouldn't feel crowded, but close enough so a step or two would put him within touching distance.

"I—I couldn't stay," she told him, lifting her chin. "With your sight back, you don't . . . don't—"

"Need you?" he supplied. "Want you? Love you?"

Julia's heart seemed to stop. Her breath caught at the top of her throat. She felt cheeks flame, then grow pale.

"L-love—?" she repeated shakily. Emerson had said as much to her, of course. But except for one euphoric moment of foolishness, she hadn't permitted herself to think about the possibility that her feelings might be requited. She told herself she couldn't think about it now, either.

But why would he say . . . ? she asked herself.

Because he doesn't know the truth, came the brutal reply.

"With all my heart," Royce said simply.

"No." She shook her head, her fair, heavy hair shifting around her face. "You can't. You don't. Royce, you d-don't *know . . .* "

"I know I owe you an apology for turning my back on a girl named Juline Fischer more than ten years ago."

The world started to spin. Julia swayed, her vision blurring. She closed her eyes. A split second later she felt Royce's arms around her. She resisted the contact for the space of a heartbeat. He tightened his hold, almost as though trying to reassure her the comfort he was offering wouldn't be withdrawn, no matter what. Unable to pull back, she gave herself up to his embrace. It felt like a homecoming.

"Shh, sweetheart," Royce murmured, caressing her with slow, soothing strokes. "Shh. It's all right. Everything's finally all right."

She lifted her head, her hair spilling back from her face. Blue-green eyes searched dark ones and found nothing but tenderness. "Did . . . did Emerson tell you?"

Royce nodded, his warm, strong hands still moving over her in a gentle rhythm. "And Dennis." His lips twisted for an instant. "I wish it had been you."

She looked away. "I couldn't."

"I understand."

There was silence. Julia forced herself to bring her gaze back to Royce's face. She was still afraid to believe that he'd accepted the truth about her with such equanimity. Dear Lord, when she looked back...

"How can you say you love me?" she asked tautly. "If Emerson and Dennis told you...if you know what I am—"

Royce lifted one hand and pressed his fingertips to her lips. "How can I not say what's true?" he demanded softly. "And as for the other, I know *who* you are, Julia. I also know *what* you did, a long time ago. I'm not going to say the past doesn't matter. I hate that there were people who hurt you. I thank God there were others who helped. But as strong as those feelings about other people are, they're nothing compared with my feelings about you. I love you, sweetheart. I love you, and I want to make a life with you."

She was shaking like a leaf in a windstorm, finally beginning to believe. "Are you asking—?"

Royce cupped her face in his palms, his expression solemn. There was an emotion in his eyes she couldn't put a name to at first. Then she realized it was uncertainty. Uncertainty about *her.*

He doesn't know, she thought, stunned. He doesn't know I love him!

"If what happened between us during the past month was a matter of...gratitude...on your part, please, tell me," he said. The effort he was expending to keep his voice steady was palpable. "But if it was *more*..."

"More?" Julia repeated as his voice trailed off. Her feelings for him welled up, sweeping over her last emotional barriers, transporting her into a free and open world where everything wonderful was possible. "Oh, Royce. What we had was *everything!* Can't you see that? I *love* you! I love you so m-much."

And with that, she surged up on tiptoe and kissed him with all the passion she possessed.

When the kiss finally came to an end, they were both trembling.

Long afterward, Royce told her he'd thought he'd heard a cheer from inside the house when their lips had met. Although Julia was more than willing to concede that her self-styled brothers were capable of spying on her in the name of being protective, she had no way of gauging the accuracy of Royce's claim. The only thing *she'd* heard at the time was the thunderous exultation of her full-to-the-brim heart.

Royce cupped her chin once again, his hands very gentle, his eyes very dark. "Can you forgive me for what I did to Juline Fischer?" he asked huskily.

Julia blinked. "Forgive you?"

He nodded.

She blinked again, struggling to make sense of the question. "Why—what's to *forgive?* Royce, you saved my life!"

"But I left you."

"You did more for me in one night than— *Don't you understand?* It's because of you I had a second chance. It's because of you I came to live with the Kendricks. It's because of you that there's a Julia."

"No." Royce shook his head vehemently. "That's because of *you,* sweetheart. A lot of people get second chances. A lot of people waste them. They don't see what they have. But not you. Oh, no. Dear Lord, when I think about what you've done in the past ten years, what you've made of yourself..." He paused, his eyes sheening over with emotion. "I've been given a second chance, too, sweetheart. And thanks to you, I'm not blind to what that means. I walked away from you—from Juline Fischer—more than a decade ago because I didn't think there was anything more I could do for her than shell out some money for medical bills. Considering the man I was back then, I may have been right. But I'm *not* that man anymore. I'm not empty. I'm not—"

Now it was Julia's turn to shake her head. "I don't love what you aren't, Royce," she told him throatily. "I love what you *are.*"

Their eyes locked and held for several searingly sweet seconds. Then Royce exhaled on a shuddery breath and reached into the pocket of his jacket and took out a small velvet-covered box. He snapped it open. Nestled inside was a pearl ring. It was a modest piece of jewelry, yet its delicate, almost old-fashioned loveliness enchanted Julia to the very center of her soul.

"This was my mother's," Royce told her. "She gave it to me just before she died. She said she hoped I'd give it to the woman I wanted to marry once I found her."

"Oh, Royce..."

"Will you be my wife, Julia?"

"Yes. Oh, yes!"

Two weeks later Julia Kendricks became Mrs. Royce Archer Williams.

Although the ceremony was small, the amount of joy it generated was enormous.

The groom had two best men: Talley O'Hara Emerson and Dr. Dennis Mitchell.

The bride was given in marriage by her foster father, John, and her three brothers—the youngest of whom struck up an instant friendship with the older of her husband-to-be's two supporters. She was attended by her foster mother, Emily, and Nancy Hansen. Both of them cried—a lot.

As they took their vows before God and the assembled witnesses, Julia and Royce gazed deeply into each other's eyes. What they saw was a future illuminated by true love— the light that transcends all darkness.

* * * * *

Another wonderful year of romance concludes with

Christmas Memories

Share in the magic and memories of romance during the holiday season with this collection of two full-length contemporary Christmas stories, by two bestselling authors

Diana Palmer
Marilyn Pappano

Available in December at your favorite retail outlet.

MONTANA™
Mavericks

Stories that capture living and loving
beneath the Big Sky, where legends live
on...and mystery lingers.

This December, explore more MONTANA MAVERICKS with

THE RANCHER TAKES A WIFE
by Jackie Merritt

He'd made up his mind. He'd loved her almost a lifetime
and now he was going to have her, come hell or high
water.

And don't miss a minute of the loving as the passion continues with:

OUTLAW LOVERS
by Pat Warren (January)

WAY OF THE WOLF
by Rebecca Daniels (February)

THE LAW IS NO LADY
by Helen R. Myers (March)
and many more!

Only from **Silhouette®** where passion lives.

SILHOUETTE®
Desire®

MAN of the Month 1995

Don't let the winter months get you down because the heat is about to get turned way up... with the sexiest hunks of 1995!

January: *A NUISANCE*
by Lass Small

February: *COWBOYS DON'T CRY*
by Anne McAllister

March: *THAT BURKE MAN*
the 75th Man of the Month
by Diana Palmer

April: *MR. EASY*
by Cait London

May: *MYSTERIOUS MOUNTAIN*
by Annette Broadrick

June: *SINGLE DAD*
by Jennifer Greene

MAN OF THE MONTH...
ONLY FROM
SIILHOUETTE DESIRE

MOM95JJ

CHILDREN OF

series continues with
THE HEADSTRONG BRIDE
by Joan Johnston

Rancher Sam Longstreet knew Garth Whitelaw was
responsible for his family's troubles. And he set out to even
the score. Sam planned to sweep young Callie Whitelaw off
her feet and marry her. But he hadn't bargained on *loving*
his headstrong bride!

Look for *The Headstrong Bride*, book two of the
CHILDREN OF HAWK'S WAY miniseries, coming your

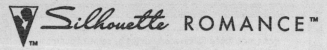
Silhouette ROMANCE™

'Tis the season for romantic bliss.
It all begins with just one kiss—

UNDER THE MISTLETOE

Celebrate the joy of the season and the thrill of romance with this special collection:

#1048 ANYTHING FOR DANNY by Carla Cassidy——Fabulous Fathers
#1049 TO WED AT CHRISTMAS by Helen R. Myers
#1050 MISS SCROOGE by Toni Collins
#1051 BELIEVING IN MIRACLES by Linda Varner——Mr. Right, Inc.
#1052 A COWBOY FOR CHRISTMAS by Stella Bagwell
#1053 SURPRISE PACKAGE by Lynn Bulock

Available in December, from Silhouette Romance.

SILHOUETTE... Where Passion Lives

Don't miss these Silhouette favorites by some of our most
distinguished authors! And now you can receive a discount by
ordering two or more titles!

SD#05786	QUICKSAND by Jennifer Greene	$2.89	☐
SD#05795	DEREK by Leslie Guccione	$2.99	☐
SD#05818	NOT JUST ANOTHER PERFECT WIFE		
	by Robin Elliott	$2.99	☐
IM#07505	HELL ON WHEELS by Naomi Horton	$3.50	☐
IM#07514	FIRE ON THE MOUNTAIN		
	by Marion Smith Collins	$3.50	☐
IM#07559	KEEPER by Patricia Gardner Evans	$3.50	☐
SSE#09879	LOVING AND GIVING by Gina Ferris	$3.50	☐
SSE#09892	BABY IN THE MIDDLE	$3.50 U.S.	☐
	by Marie Ferrarella	$3.99 CAN.	☐
SSE#09902	SEDUCED BY INNOCENCE	$3.50 U.S.	☐
	by Lucy Gordon	$3.99 CAN.	☐
SR#08952	INSTANT FATHER by Lucy Gordon	$2.75	☐
SR#08984	AUNT CONNIE'S WEDDING		
	by Marie Ferrarella	$2.75	☐
SR#08990	JILTED by Joleen Daniels	$2.75	☐

(limited quantities available on certain titles)

AMOUNT	$_____
DEDUCT: 10% DISCOUNT FOR 2+ BOOKS	$_____
POSTAGE & HANDLING	$_____
($1.00 for one book, 50¢ for each additional)	
APPLICABLE TAXES*	$_____
TOTAL PAYABLE	$_____
(check or money order—please do not send cash)	

To order, complete this form and send it, along with a check or money order
for the total above, payable to Silhouette Books, to: **In the U.S.**: 3010 Walden
Avenue, P.O. Box 9077, Buffalo, NY 14269-9077; **In Canada**: P.O. Box 636,
Fort Erie, Ontario, L2A 5X3.

Name:_____

Address:_____ City:_____

State/Prov.:_____ Zip/Postal Code:_____

*New York residents remit applicable sales taxes.
Canadian residents remit applicable GST and provincial taxes.　　SBACK-DF

V *Silhouette*®
TM